Sins

of the

Father

Sabina Halvorsen

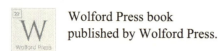

Wolford Press book
published by Wolford Press.

This book is a work of fiction. While many of the locations are based on real places, the characters, names, events, incidents, and locales are a product of the author's imagination. Any resemblance to any actual events or persons, living or dead, is purely coincidence.

Copyright © 2022 by Sabrina Halvorson

Originally published digitally and in paperback in 2022 by Wolford Press

All rights reserved, including the right to reproduce this work or any portion thereof in any form whatsoever.
For copyright information, contact the author at Sabrina@SabrinaHalvorson.com.

ISBN: 9798832223339 (paperback)
ISBN: 9798832889313 (hardcover)

First Wolford Press edition October 1, 2022

Wolford Press is a registered trademark.

Front and back cover by RebecaCovers ©Sabrina Halvorson

Images within the text © Sabrina Halvorson

For my father, who was a wonderful man.

Sins
of the
Father

Chapter 1

Sarah turned her head and looked at the sliver of light coming from under the door. It was the only part of the room she could see through the darkness and even that was dimmer now than it was just a few minutes ago.

She was used to this room. She and her sister were here every Wednesday to see the doctor and do his tests. They've been doing the tests for two years now, since Sarah was five. The tests weren't bad back then, but now, they've gotten worse. Sometimes the doctor puts tiny needles in their scalps and connects them to a machine. Sometimes they just look at pictures. Now they sleep sometimes, too. He tells them what to dream about. It was fun at first, but lately, they've been dreaming about things Sarah doesn't like. Things like monsters, or worse: The Nothing.

This night was a Nothing night and that scared her worst of all. Every time Sarah dreamed of The Nothing, her sister in the next room screamed with nightmares of Sarah's death. Sometimes, her screams would wake Sarah from her dream just as The Nothing covered her face to smother her. Tonight was different. Her sister wasn't there, so there would be no screams to wake Sarah.

Grown-ups say the dark is safe, that there's nothing in the dark that wasn't there when the lights were on, Sarah thought. She tried again to look around the room.

But, that's not true.

She was only seven years old, but Sarah felt it coming, the tightness in her stomach that wouldn't go away. If she went to sleep, she would never wake up. Still, sleep was coming. Sarah's eyes watered as she struggled to keep them open. Her heavy lids blinked down and shot open again as she fought against the injection the doctor gave her earlier. She strained to hear the usual murmurs of her mother in the hallway, just beyond the door, but there was only silence and the amplified drumming of her heartbeat inside her ears.

Eyes closed.

Where do we go when we sleep?

Eyes open.

We go to The Nothing. We wake up when The Nothing lets us out.

Eyes closed.

Sometimes, it doesn't let us out.

Please open, eyes.

She wasn't strong enough.

The cold in the room bit at her skin and she tried to pull up the blanket that covered her legs. Nothing happened. Her arms wouldn't move. Not even her fingers would wiggle. Sarah tried to scream, but no sound came out. It wouldn't have mattered anyway.

No one would save her.

Sleep was coming.

The Nothing was coming.

Sarah's body was heavy, and panic swelled in her throat. Her heart should be racing, but she felt it strangely slow and methodic in her chest. The steady rhythm pulsed her deeper into rest. Her mind blurred as her body relaxed. Her only bit of hope, the dim light under the door, grew dark and the stinging scent of the sterile room stopped hurting her nostrils.

That's when it came for her.

The Nothing.

It started in her feet, which could no longer feel the cold, then crept up numb legs. It swallowed her with its deepness, and she couldn't fight against its pull. A final struggle for breath, and her little body went limp on the bed.

Sarah gave in to The Nothing.

This time, it wouldn't let her out.

Washington, D.C.

"When our bodies are done living, we return to the void. Not in body and not in mind, but, rather, in consciousness. There is no thinking in the void, simply awareness. Though, awareness is anything but simple. Awareness is everything."

Dr. Jackson Cole stood sweating on a stage in front of dozens of tables filled with potential donors to his foundation. They were a blur of blank faces and dark blue suits appropriate for the midday luncheon. Jackson's forehead creased as he searched for the words that would get them to stop staring and start listening. He doubted they would ever understand, but that didn't matter. He swallowed his contempt and continued.

"Our entire reality depends on how we are aware of it. If you are aware of pain, your reality is painful. If you are aware of misery, your reality is miserable. If you are aware of beauty, your reality is beautiful. So, consider this," he paused for effect, "You create your individual reality from your individual awareness. Further, since we each have a different awareness, or a different reality, I would say that there is no one true reality."

Jackson saw the shine of perfectly groomed white hair from the nearest table as a man lowered his gaze. He knew the look all too well. It was his father, and he wore his discrete expression of embarrassment. Jackson brandished his next words like a silver dagger.

"Humans have studied awareness in one way or another for as long as we've been alive. Our foundation strives to make that a *scientific* study, rather than the desperate fantasies of those who lack vision. With your help, we can start to truly understand the capabilities of the human consciousness."

Jackson bowed his head in appreciation of the polite applause. He was anxious to leave the event and get back to work. Still, bound by responsibility and appropriateness, he resolved to make small talk with the distinguished guests with the hope that it would open their checkbooks. His only genuine smile came at the thought that these people couldn't imagine the experiments they were really funding.

"Another fine speech, son." His father's tone was especially cool today.

Jackson shook his father's hand and matched the emotional disconnect. "Thank you for your continued support of important research, doctor."

The exchange was brief, but it was all Jackson could take. Before the salad course was served, he slipped out the side door and headed outside.

He pulled his coat closed and cursed the chill that was too crisp for D.C. in September. He normally enjoyed the brisk air, but today it was tedious. His nightmares had returned, and he was getting less sleep with each passing night. They were the lucid memory dreams that still clung to him from the harshness of his youth.

His father, with his high-profile medical practice, was publicly loved and respected, always calm, and friendly. He was a different person at home. Never physically abusive to Jackson, but angry and hurtful. He was a miserable man and required everyone around him to be as miserable as he was. Jackson's mother tried to compensate for her husband's bitterness. She was soft and gentle and worked to make the world better. Her volunteer work had earned her as much love and respect as her husband enjoyed, but Jackson knew she deserved so much more because her kindness was real.

The son of two people so often in the spotlight, there was little choice for Jackson but to become as much a public figure as they were. His father laid out the plan early in Jackson's life. He would come into his father's general medical practice as an employee, then a partner, and one day take over the business.

He wanted to be a physicist.

His father didn't approve.

Despite years of bullying from his own father, Jackson graduated top of his class at MIT and became a doctor in his own right, though not the medical doctor his father wanted. Jackson now led a science research foundation that explored experimental physics. He still felt like the puppet in his father's play, however. He smiled and did interviews on how scientific research advances the medical field and often found a way to speak kindly of his father's medical practice. Even at 44 years old, he was forever the dutiful son. As such, there would never be freedom for Jackson. Even trapped by his name, Jackson would always be Jack's son.

San Francisco

The glow of the morning sun just crested the horizon as the city awakened from its few short hours of relative stillness. Soon, San Francisco would be alive with the chaos of millions of lives intermingling, each struggling with the importance of its individual needs.

Thomas inhaled a deep breath as he kept his temper in check. It was only 7 a.m. and already the freeway was bumper to bumper. He dialed his wife and connected his phone to the car Bluetooth. She answered with a question.

"Stuck at work?"

"No, stuck on the freeway. It was a rough night. Can you take the morning bus stop run with the kid? I want to go to mass and clear my head."

She agreed and Thomas hung up just in time to avoid rear-ending the car in front of him as traffic stopped yet again. He would be late for the 7:30 mass at St. Mary's Cathedral. He considered skipping it, but Catholic guilt was alive in him, and his daily mass routine helped keep it at bay. It also helped to clear his mind of the tragedies he saw as an overnight emergency room doctor. Just a few hours ago he had stabilized a teenager with a bullet in his thigh. The boy had long, unwashed hair and dirty clothes. He was likely one of the hundreds of homeless people who made their way through the city streets and often fell victim to senseless violence. Thomas had seen it too many times, and it seemed the patients kept getting younger. Thomas, on the other hand, felt older with each passing emergency room shift.

A glance at himself in the rearview mirror reinforced that feeling. The light blond hair of his youth had darkened with age and now was starting to lighten up again in patches of silver by each temple. At 36 years old, he was young for graying hair. He didn't mind, though. His wife said it made him look distinguished. He told himself the same was true for the lines starting to form at the outer corners of his eyes. Thomas sighed and made a mental note to add an instance of vanity to his weekly confession.

A short time later, he walked into the beautiful cathedral. He smiled as he thought to himself that it was an act of God that he got there in time for the entrance song. He dipped his fingers in the basin of holy water and made the sign of the cross before heading to his usual spot in the back of the room, kneeling to the alter, and sidestepping into the pew. The church was dotted with a scattering of attendees today, most of whom sang softly and shyly together a song from the hymnal. A few others held the book and mumbled sounds in an effort to appear as if they were singing. Thomas fit in neither category. His rich baritone resonated in the back half of the church. He sang with gusto, even if he was, on occasion, off-key.

"The Lord be with you," the priest greeted the church.

"And with your spirit," united voices returned.

Thomas's tired body stood tall with reverence. His back was straight and firm, his chin slightly raised, as the weight of his work lifted. He felt calm here. It recharged him. He knew what it felt like to be filled with the Holy Spirit. It was this, the gentle tightness of anticipation in his chest and calm elation in his mind. It gave him strength and at the same time, it gave him peace. Thomas had spent his life with a fear he had never admitted. He was afraid to be alone. Coming to church reminded him that he would never be alone, as God was always with him.

By the time he had consumed the body of Christ and said the final prayers, he was ready to head back out into the chaos of life.

Minnesota

It was the calm that drew her here. There were few places left in the United States where a person could live a quiet existence, as removed from the fastness of the world as they cared to be. When Aurea found her rural Minnesota home five years ago, her requirements had been few but non-negotiable: Plenty of land between neighbors, a very low cost of living, and decent internet access. After all, she was a recluse, not a hermit, and even a recluse needed to stay connected.

She hadn't always lived a solitary life. She built up her savings dealing in real estate on California's Central Coast. Her uncanny instinct for matching the right buyer with the right property, coupled with hard work and determination, earned her evenings of fine wine and ocean sunsets, parties with live music and flowing champagne, and the occasional Armani suit crumpled on her floor.

It was all a world away now. Rather than the sand on the beach, it was the soft crunch of fallen leaves beneath her steps. No longer showing houses, she wrote articles about real estate for a news website. The champagne flute was now a steaming coffee cup, and instead of handsome lovers in expensive suits, she had the company of a cat, a dog, and several chickens she hoped to keep alive. The fast life had always been a means to an end; the loud, hurried path to this peaceful solitude where she felt protected from the world but still endlessly enshrouded in the energy of it. That energy was the secret to her success. It always had been. She knew that one day it would be her downfall.

She had sensed the energy for as long as she could remember. As a child, she called the two sides of the energy the light and the dark. Her mother was a gifted woman, still, she had never felt their presence. Not like Aurea did. When Aurea was young, the darkness faded in and out while the light blossomed. Now, the light was simply steady as the dark grew stronger.

She sought out the darkness this morning as she lay with her eyes closed, mind clear, and body relaxed on the carpeted floor. The rich scent of clove incense teased her senses as she let herself drift into deep meditation. Soon, she walked in the memory of him, as she often did.

His smile was broad and friendly, his hand strong as it gripped hers in a greeting. Aurea was struck with sensations as their hands connected. Her intuition was finely tuned, and

Aurea always trusted it. It was their first introduction, but she knew his energy. They were connected. Did he feel it, too?

"Aurea is an unusual name. Tell me about it," he said to her.

"It's unusual here, but in other cultures, it's more common," Aurea explained. "I was named after Saint Aurea of Spain, who was known for her many miracles and visions."

"That's a lot to live up to."

Aurea relaxed into a smile. "I'm sure you know something of that, too."

He raised his wine glass in agreement and nodded. "That, I do."

The brief conversation was nine years ago, and it lasted only a minute before the man was whisked off for more introductions. It was a charity fundraising event aboard an extravagant yacht. Aurea nearly turned down the invitation, but intuition told her she needed to be there. As she gazed out at the gold and amber sunset reflecting off the San Francisco Bay, she knew it wasn't just the view she was destined to discover here. She had just connected with the dark half of the energy she knew so well but could never quite identify. It now had a name: Jackson Cole.

Her brother.

Since that meeting, Aurea kept watch over the man from afar. He was in the news on occasion, so it wasn't hard to see what he was up to publicly. His private life was a different story. Aside from the fact that he was a dedicated scientist, there wasn't much said about him. He seemed quite tame and even a bit boring. Aurea's instincts told her that perceptions like that are often wrong.

Aurea was taught to trust her instincts at a young age. She grew up in a small California coastal town, popular with surfers and tourists passing through on their way to resort areas. She lived with her mother in a small house next to a storefront where her mother sold crystals, herbs from their garden, and a collection of books on mystical religions. Aurea had never met her father and her mother never talked about him. It was as if he simply didn't exist. Aurea had little curiosity about the other half of her parentage. Why be interested in someone who had never shown interest in her?

She was in junior high when she started to understand the light and darkness she occasionally felt. When she felt the dark as a child, she slipped into moody sadness. When she felt the light, she was giddy. As she grew to understand more about her own feelings, she came to realize that these times of light and dark were not coming from within her. She was sensing them from some distant place outside of her.

"Like when we're listening to the radio and another station bleeds in just a little," her mother once explained. Aurea was twelve then and ready to go beyond childhood understanding. "You have an antenna that is very good, very sensitive, and you can pick up far away stations that you don't even know about."

That was when Aurea's studies in the metaphysical world began with her mother as her guide.

"There's so much discourse between them, but still, the world's religions have many similar beliefs about the universe and the divine," her mother explained one misty day on the beach. She gathered shells and laid them in rows as she spoke.

"Christianity, Islam, and Judaism all share a common origin. The Virgin Mary and Christ, the Son of God, are both often thought to be distinctly Christian, but they also appear in various ways in Muslim and Hindu teachings." She moved two shells from one row to another and continued moving them as she spoke to show the connections. "The Hindu god Krishna is part of the Hindu theistic trinity, which is similar to the Christian trinity. An incarnation of Krishna, known as Vishnu, is compared to the Christian Son of God. It is believed he will come back to Earth one final time and restore the balance between good and evil. There are also similarities between Hinduism and Judaism, such as using a special language for prayer or not eating certain foods."

"When we take out what is different, and instead look at what is the same, we start to see beyond the veil of humanity's natural ego," she softly explained. "Rather than how one or the other is better, we focus instead on what they together show us: We are all connected. It is there that we begin to understand the connection we have to all of existence. In our teachings, we call it the Akashic field. It is everything."

Though she felt so far away now, Aurea often remembered her mother during her meditations. She strained to hear her mother's voice, to always remember the warm velvet tone of it. As much as it brought joy, the memory of her mother brought turmoil and shame. Her mother believed strongly in the things she taught Aurea, but when Aurea was in her early 20s, she wanted desperately to fit into the mainstream. She worked to change the core of who she was and started by abandoning her mother's teachings. She still loved her mother deeply, but secretly Aurea feared being associated with her. Aurea was building a professional reputation for herself, and even in the most liberal parts of

California's coastline, pagan naturalists were not well respected within the business community.

It didn't matter now. Aurea felt a tear dampen her face as it rolled into her hair. She knew now how wrong she had been. Her mother was gone, and everything was gone with her. The house, the store, her smile, her musical laugh, the scent of lavender in her hair, it was all gone. Aurea would never get back the time she spent wishing her mother was different and trying to fit into a world that would never love her as much as her mother did.

Now, she didn't want to fit in. She wanted to be every bit as vibrant and captivating as her mother was. She wanted to see the things her mother saw and know the things her mother knew. When she tried, all she felt was unending emptiness.

After some time, she forced the memory of her mother aside and let Jackson slip back into her thoughts. She couldn't shake the question of why he was so strongly on her mind lately, and why she often imagined him surrounded by children.

Washington, D.C.

There are things that some scientists do anonymously to avoid ridicule. Research into things like UFOs, paranormal activity, and psychic abilities is on the list. Jackson did nothing anonymously. He did, however, do things secretly.

His work in quantum physics earned him some whispers behind his back, but given his social status, no one dared say anything too loudly. His family contributed to several scientific organizations, and those donations allowed Jackson some leeway within the foundation. The leeway he appreciated the most was that he was often ignored by his coworkers.

They were ignoring him that afternoon as a study participant came for an interview. Not a head bothered to turn as he led the woman down the plain white hallway to his office at the end. He held the door open and motioned for her to sit in the chair across from his desk.

"You have a lot of awards," she said as she sat. He nodded in acknowledgment. His walls were decorated with various accolades, some earned, some bought with donations. "You don't have any pictures of your family."

"I've dedicated my life to this foundation. I don't have a family," Jackson said as he softened his expression and gave a friendly smile. It didn't come naturally; He had practiced the look in the mirror for years. "Let's talk about your family. Your son did very well on the initial test, and I'd like to have him come in tonight for another."

"Does he get paid again?"

"Yes, he'll make two hundred dollars tonight," Jackson said. From the look of the woman's threadbare coat and worn shoes, he assumed it would be a tempting offer.

"That's a lot more than last time. What are you guys doing tonight?"

"You'll be with him the whole time. Here, look through these." Jackson handed a folder of drawings across the desk to her. As she flipped through them, he explained. "I am repeating an experiment that other scientists have done for years, but while many of them have studied adults, I study children. I monitor reaction time as the brain focuses on those prints you're holding. They're called ambiguous pictures. Pick one and look at it."

Sins of the Father   15

She opened the folder and looked at the white page with a black design running down the middle.

"Now, focus on the black ink. You'll eventually see the shape of a candlestick. If you switch and focus on the white paper, you'll see two faces looking at each other." He watched her reaction as her perception of the image changed. "The idea is that the brain can only see one image at a time. I monitor how long it takes the brain to focus on one image or the other, as well as the time it took to switch from one to the other."

"Why is that important?" the woman asked as she flipped to another picture.

"From there, I can study how the brain works in selecting which image to see, which areas of the brain are involved, and other various brain functions." He didn't tell her the rest.

Jackson took the experiment even further. He aimed to prove that the brain is capable of seeing both images at once by activating a more intricate quantum process within the cells. Not only that, but once a brain knew how to use that intricate process, it could interact with other brains that operated at that advanced level.

That's where he lost the faith of other scientists.

He didn't care. Advancements weren't made by everyone agreeing with each other.

"It won't hurt?"

"No, he'll be wearing something like a hat that has sensors in it to record his brain function. It's no worse than a piece of tape." Jackson sensed that she was just about ready to give her permission. "I can give you half the payment right now if you like."

As he suspected, that got him the confirmation that she and her son would return at eight that evening. As he walked the woman out, she asked why he was conducting the experiment so late.

"This way there's nothing else going on in the lab. It helps if there are no distractions," he told her. In truth, he scheduled the study for after his coworkers were gone for the day because he didn't want an audience of other researchers, especially those who don't respect what he was working on. While other researchers in the foundation studied the workings of quantum mechanics, Jackson studied the possibilities of quantum consciousness.

He hated how mystical it sounded when the study of quantum consciousness was quite scientific. It studied how the thought process works through quantum mechanics, which is the way cells interact with each other. Humans have studied consciousness for much of history. However, it wasn't until the 1990s that the first detailed theory of quantum consciousness was made by notable scientists, one a physicist and the other an anesthesiologist. The physicist has a list of awards the length of his arm, including a Nobel Prize in Physics and an esteemed mathematical award that he shares with Stephen Hawking. The anesthesiologist also holds several awards, including being named on the Best Doctors in America list several times. Though their theory was met with some criticism and has been updated through the years, Jackson considered them pioneers in his field and two of the few people in the world he admired. He had attended conferences and speaking engagements by each of the scientists but had yet to meet either. He feared letting them down. They had done so much, and he had yet to publish anything substantial.

He also knew they would not approve of some of his practices. It was very difficult to study the human brain while the human was still using it, yet nearly impossible to study if the brain was no longer alive within the human. That was just one of the challenges to studying consciousness. There are many more.

Jackson was pulled from his thoughts as his cell phone rang. He pulled it from his pocket and glanced at the caller ID, then closed the door behind the woman and hurried to answer before the call went to voicemail.

"Hello. Do you have good news for me?" he asked.

"I do."

"Well?"

"He's perfect."

Chapter 2

Adam's ears filled with the fast, wild pace of his heart that beat nearly as fast and loud as his running footsteps. The shadow of a monster he couldn't quite see raced behind him so close the beast's heavy, hot breath landed, wet, on Adams's back. He knew he shouldn't, but he couldn't stop himself from craning his neck to see what chased him. He could feel it just inches behind him, but his eyes showed him nothing.

"Adam," a woman's voice echoed. The sound came from somewhere in the darkness. Not behind him, not in front of him, just somewhere. It was soft and gentle, a contradiction to his panic. "Don't look at it, Adam. Just keep going."

Then she was gone. He didn't know how he knew she was gone, but she certainly was. He was alone again with the monster that hunted him. It wanted him, and he felt it was near, though he still couldn't see it. Adam was blind in the dark and terrified of what filled the blackness with him. Some classmates had teased him about being afraid of the dark. He was eight years old now and should have outgrown his fear. But they didn't know that sometimes the things we can't see in the dark are truly dangerous monsters, even in the light.

Adam knew.

San Francisco

Susan Brown smiled and turned the page on her daily schedule. The start of another day meant she was another day closer to finishing her task and going home. It certainly wasn't glamorous being a school counselor. In truth, Susan didn't like the assignment. She had respect for the people who were called to work with kids, but she wasn't one of them. She liked her life as a research psychologist. It was her way of making the future better. But this chore was only for a few months. It probably took her longer to go through the hiring process than she'll be in the job. Jackson promised it wouldn't be for long.

The thought of him made her ivory-complected face flush pink with heat. He was the smartest person Susan had ever known and she was eager for the opportunity to work closely with him once again. It didn't hurt that she found him extremely attractive with his tall, sturdy build, jet-black hair, and icy blue eyes just like his father's.

Susan had first met Jackson through his father. She and the older man had shared a brief tryst when she was studying psychology in grad school. It was exciting at first but took an unexpected turn as things progressed and ended with tears and devastating heartbreak for Susan. Jack, ever cool and stoic, was emotionally unaffected. He later wanted to pay for her silence with cash and the promise of a job at his son's science foundation.

She turned down the cash.

"Hey, want to go check on the kids?" Susan looked up and saw Principal Romero standing in the doorway of her office. He was a kind-hearted man who Susan suspected was well past retirement age. Since the first day of school, they had enjoyed a daily walk through the halls as the kids headed to class.

"I thought you'd never ask," Susan said with a smile. She enjoyed the routine and the conversations they had. The one good thing about her assignment was that she got to be whoever she wanted to be. Nobody knew her here, and she was to keep it that way. She got to create her own backstory, and she made it nothing like her reality. Anyone could search for information on her over the internet but being a research psychologist didn't give her a very glamorous life. There wasn't much to find.

They walked through the school and made small talk about their plans for the upcoming weekend. Susan kept her comments vague so she wouldn't have to remember what she said. The swarm of activity and noise surrounded her and made it impossible for her to focus on anything. The halls were filled with children running to catch up with friends or shouting at each other, hurried parents trying to say goodbye and head to their own busy lives, and teachers working to keep the chaos to a minimum. The elementary school itself was a generic institution afforded by taxpayers. It reminded Susan of the school she attended as a child with butcher paper decorations that adorned the doors, floors that were always at least a little sticky, and the scent of something almost recognizable coming from the cafeteria.

She took a deep breath and brushed a wavy lock of her amber-colored hair behind her ear. It was a nervous tick she'd had for as long as she could remember. Stroking her hair reminded her of easy afternoons sitting cross-legged and watching Sesame Street while her sister sat behind her and brushed Susan's unruly curls. They were her favorite times with her big sister. Even now, she could swear she smelled the hint of peppermint chewing gum her sister loved so much. Susan never chewed gum anymore. Still, the echo of the scent lingered in the air.

Susan gave a small shiver and pulled her thoughts back to the busy hallway. Her sister was gone, but there was another child she needed to find. He was the entire reason she was in San Francisco, working a job she would normally hate in a place that was her personal torment: a building filled with kids.

She spotted him, the one kid she enjoyed being around, walking alone in the hall with one shoe untied and his backpack securely over his shoulders.

"Hey there. How's your morning going?" she asked as he passed by.

"Pretty good," he said with a shrug. "I had strawberry Pop-Tarts this morning."

"If I remember correctly, that's your favorite." Susan swept the boy's hair out of his eyes. "Do you want to come for a chat today?"

"Can I come during math?"

"Sure, but just this once." Susan smiled down at him. "I'll send a note to your teacher. See you later, Adam."

Susan watched him walk off to his classroom as the principal came to her side and leaned close.

"You're not supposed to have favorites, you know," he whispered.

Susan glanced sideways at him and saw his friendly smile.

"Everyone has favorites," she said. "You're just not supposed to let anyone know."

"True. You must be a very good therapist," he said with a laugh, then turned his head to look around.

"Did you lose something?" Susan asked.

"No, I was just wondering where that smell was coming from," he said as he continued walking.

"What smell?"

He glanced over his shoulder to reply. "Peppermint. Do you smell it?"

Susan's throat went dry, and her body turned cold. The scent was sickly-sweet like discarded candy. *Or gum*. Her hand instinctively reached to smooth the lock of hair by her ear but instead, she pinched a few of the silky strands between her fingers and pulled. She didn't bother to look as the strands of the wavy amber silk floated down past her palm and rested on the scuffed tile floor.

Several blocks away, Dr. Thomas Hernandez kissed his wife and hung his windbreaker on the coat rack by the door.

"How was the morning?" he asked her.

"Another wet one."

Thomas nodded with understanding. "It's probably just a phase. A lot of kids go through this."

"I know. That's what you keep saying. But, there's this website that says if bedwetting starts suddenly, it could be a sign of a problem."

"Amanda," Thomas took his wife's hands in his, "do you know how many years I spent in medical school? We're not going to become those parents who get their medical knowledge from the internet. I can't stand those parents."

Amanda let out a breath and rolled her eyes before looking into her husband's again. "Sometimes the internet's right."

"Fine. Yes, I concede. It could be a sign of a problem. *Could*," Thomas emphasized at Amanda's triumphant expression. "The pediatrician says medically, Adam's fine. We have him talking to the school psychologist. What do you want to do next?"

Amanda reached into her back pocket and pulled out a folded piece of paper that she handed to Thomas.

"There's this sleep study that Susan recommended. She said she could get him in next weekend."

"Susan?"

"Ms. Brown. From the school."

"I know who she is," Thomas said. "How are you already on a first-name basis with her?"

"Thomas, stop. You're grasping for anything to be irritated about."

He knew she was right, and that made him even more irritated. He took a slow, deep breath and relaxed his shoulders. He took another deep breath for good measure and wrapped his arms around his wife's waist.

"Adam's getting used to the idea of being a big brother. I'm sure by the time baby brother is born, he will be back to his usual self. It's just three more months now," he said and kissed Amanda's forehead in an apology. "I'd like to look at this with a clear head, after some rest. Let me sleep on the sleep study?"

"I swear, if you weren't so handsome, I'd kick you out."

"Don't forget charming," Thomas teased. "And a doctor. It's like you cast a spell for the perfect man."

Amanda rolled her eyes again. "Go to bed. And don't joke about witchcraft. It's from the devil and I won't have anything evil in this house."

Minnesota

"Don't be afraid of the Devil card." The gray-haired woman kept her focus on the Tarot cards in front of her as she spoke.

"I'm not," Aurea answered. She sat at the woman's table out of compassion more than anything else. She regularly read her own cards and was confident in her interpretations. But, as she walked through the hall of the Minneapolis hotel's conference center, she noticed no one else would even look at the woman sitting at her folding table with a simple cloth thrown over it. The conference attendees were drawn to the decorated booths with shining crystals and heavily scented incense for sale. The conference on spirituality brought a kaleidoscope of people together.

"People tend to think it's something bad when the Devil shows up in a reading. Do you read cards?"

"I do. My mother taught me," Aurea said, the familiar twinge of hurt and guilt curling around in her chest. "The deck I use doesn't have a Devil, but I remember some from my mother's teachings. Tell me what it means to you."

"The Devil represents the darker side of ourselves and the attachment we have to it. It's the want for material things or the addiction to something that hurts us. It can also show that someone is living in fear of something or that there is a dark shadow on your life. But do you see where it's at?" The woman tapped on the table. "This is the position of your past, so the darkness is either in your past or something from your past. Let's see how the other cards affect it."

Aurea watched as the woman placed a card to the right of the Devil. She was well enough versed to know it had a strong negative tone but hoped the reader would have a different interpretation. The wrinkles in the woman's forehead deepened.

"The middle card is your current situation." She tapped on the card that showed an illustration of lightning striking and cracking a castle tower, a woman falling from the window. "The Tower. It's a card of destruction and change. An upheaval. Sudden and difficult change."

She placed a third card on the table next to the Tower. Death.

"Don't worry," she patted Aurea's hand, "This doesn't mean physical death. Like the Tower, it's also a card of change. Something ending and something new beginning. This card is in the position representing your nearby future, the next few months."

Aurea looked at the three cards on the table.

"The future looks pretty grim," she said.

"Well, let's look at this all together." The woman placed both wrinkled hands on the cards in front of her and closed her eyes. Usually, Aurea would call that "showbiz mysticism", like the flashy T.V. preacher nearly passing out as he healed someone. In this old woman, with her demure cotton dress, frizzy gray hair, and the single silver and moonstone ring on her right hand, Aurea sensed sincerity. She waited quietly until the woman spoke again. "There is a darkness in your past, something you've kept at a distance. It's an unseen force, working even now, in a way that will alter your life. Hard times and changes are coming. Be prepared, but don't live in fear."

Easier said than done, Aurea thought. She regretted sitting down at the woman's table.

"There is one card left," the woman said. "It goes above the other three. Think of this card as an umbrella over your life. Not your past, your present, or your future, but your *entirety*. A strength you pull from, or a problem you keep stumbling on."

Aurea's stomach tightened as the woman pulled the card from the top of the deck. It was a beautifully drawn nightscape with the light of a silvery full moon illuminating trees in a forest. Aurea was drawn to the ethereal image.

"The Moon." The woman's creased forehead relaxed as she looked at the card. "You are a very spiritual woman, or, I should say, very connected to the spiritual nature of things. There is a veil draped between this experience and the other. Most people never see past the veil. For them, it's a wall."

She touched Aurea's hand again before going on. "You not only see past the veil, but you can go through it when you choose. I think the warning here is to not take that for granted or you'll go through it one too many times and be lost in the darkness."

The words lingered as the women stared silently at the cards on the table, each so lost in their thoughts and private interpretations that they both startled as a third woman walked up and spoke.

"I hope I'm not interrupting. It looked like you were done," she said.

"No, perfect timing," the old woman answered. She smiled at Aurea. "I always get hungry after a good reading, and this is my lunch date."

"Of course. Thank you for the information," Aurea said as she stood. She looked at the woman who joined them. She was a Native American woman, with a round face, deep brown eyes, and short, neat, black hair salted with white strands. "Wait, you're one of the speakers. The Native American religion expert from Rapid City. I saw your picture in the program."

"I am." She held out her hand. "I'm Nahimana Running Deer. You can call me Nan."

Aurea shook her hand. "Aurea Clark. I'm excited to meet you. Your session is why I decided to come to the conference. It sounded incredibly interesting."

"I think it is. Join us for lunch and I'll give you a free preview."

"I'd like that."

The old woman at the table smiled slightly and shuffled her Tarot cards. She watched the cards as she spoke. "Why don't you two go on and I'll catch up later. I think I'd prefer a quick nap."

Aurea sensed there was some matchmaking going on. She didn't mind; It was an interesting prospect, and Nan was quite attractive. She discreetly placed a twenty-dollar bill on the table to pay the woman for the reading. "Thank you for your insight. I never caught your name."

"I'm Rebecca."

Aurea stumbled slightly. It was a common name but hearing it now from this woman nearly made her weak. "That was my mother's name."

The woman just smiled and dipped her head in a fraction of a nod.

Aurea felt a little dazed as she headed to the hotel restaurant with Nan. *Probably just low blood sugar.* She ordered a salad with a glass of merlot and enjoyed the sparks of exploration as she and Nan talked.

Washington, D.C.

Jackson placed another picture in front of the boy and watched the data on the computer screen. Information scrolled in numbers, words, and lines, as the cells in the child's brain fired. He knew he was right about this one. The boy's eyes flicked between the white and black images while the numbers already showed a faster response than Jackson had seen in other children. They tested for thirty minutes before the boy's response time started dragging. It was close to the child's bedtime, and there was an expected level of mental fatigue. It did no good to continue testing.

"I think it's time for a rest. You've done very well this evening," he told the boy. He would use the boy's name, but he'd already forgotten it. In the notes before him, the boy was simply Subject B31. Like a bingo number. Officially it was to keep all subjects anonymous, but in truth, it was just easier to not know anyone's name. It made them too human, and that was always a detriment.

Jackson gave the remaining half of the payment to the boy's mother and said he'd call to set up another appointment. He was unsure of his schedule for the next few days. After they left, he went over his notes from that evening and organized them for his files. It was nearly 9 in the evening when his phone rang. Six on the West Coast. He took a breath and forced a smile. She wouldn't see the smile, but there was something to the idea that people can hear a smile through the phone. Jackson wanted to keep Susan happy.

"Good evening. How's it going out west?"

"You sound happy. The boy did well?"

"He did. The numbers are exciting. How about you? Any progress?"

"Yes," Susan's voice was rushed with excitement. It reminded Jackson of a puppy with a wagging tail, climbing up its master's leg to return the ball that was thrown. "They're going to do it. Can you be here next weekend? It's costing a pretty penny, but I talked an established sleep study location into renting you a couple of rooms. They were very happy to be mentioned in your research in exchange."

Jackson gave the puppy a treat. "You've done very well. I knew I could count on you."

Through Susan's silence, he imagined her blushing, the way she did so often when he complimented her. He found it irritating.

Still, he needed her right now to do a job that only she could, and therefore he would keep flattering her and letting her believe that he was interested.

And when he didn't need her anymore, he'd put the puppy down. After all, that's what he'd promised to do.

San Francisco

Thomas watched in some amazement as Adam dipped what had to be his hundredth French fry in ketchup and popped it in his mouth.

"I'm thoroughly impressed, not that you *can* eat so many fries, but that you want to," he said with a smile.

"They have the best fries here," Adam said, his eyes wide with excitement. "I know this place is usually for tourists, but I'm glad we came."

The pair sat at an outdoor table at a restaurant on Pier 39, one of the city's very popular tourist destinations. A couple dozen shops and a handful of restaurants made up the pier and visitors enjoyed their shopping and dining with a view of the infamous Alcatraz Island prison. Thomas avoided the pier and all the people, but he had let Adam choose their dinner. He did so knowing exactly where Adam would choose.

"I'm glad we came, too, kiddo," Thomas said as he stole a fry from Adam's plate. He'd already finished the clam chowder he ordered. "We should stop at the chocolate shop and get something for mom."

"Yeah, mom says the baby loves chocolate," Adam said with a shrug. "But I think it's just an excuse to have as much chocolate as she wants."

"Here's some advice from your father," Thomas said. "There are some things you never say to a pregnant woman, and that's one of them."

Adam nodded his head, then was thoughtful for a second. "Here's some advice from your son. Ice cream makes a very good dessert."

Thomas laughed and shook his head. He always looked forward to their weekly "guy-time" dinners when he could connect with his son and not worry about anything else. It was one appointment he never canceled. The only rule of the evening was that they never talked about anything difficult during these times. He didn't want Adam to start dreading their time together.

An hour later they drove across town, with bags of chocolate and bellies full of ice cream, and Thomas decided to break the rule, just this once.

"Hey buddy, you know that sleep study mom and I told you about earlier?" He tested the water before going further.

"Yeah."

"What do you think about it?" Thomas glanced in the rearview mirror to Adam sitting in the back seat.

Adam shrugged. "It sounds kind of weird, but kind of fun."

"So, you don't mind it then?"

"Will it hurt?" Adam asked.

"No. They stick these sensors on you that help monitor things, like how deeply you're sleeping. They stick on. No needles," Thomas kept his explanation simple. He still wasn't sold on the idea, but he didn't want that to come across to Adam.

"And you'll be there?"

"Of course."

"All night?" Adam looked at him in the rearview mirror.

"All night." Thomas looked into his son's eyes. "I'll always be there for you, buddy. I promise."

"Thanks, dad."

Thomas felt better knowing that Adam wasn't worried about the study. Still, he felt anxiety over it. He had plenty of experience with worried parents before a child's medical procedure, but it was strange for him to be on this side of the situation. Next weekend couldn't come soon enough.

Chapter 3

Adam was afraid to go to sleep. He was always afraid to go to sleep, but this time it was worse. He was in a doctor's office that was made to look like a bedroom but was still very much a doctor's office. It smelled like rubbing alcohol and a machine in the corner near his bed beeped every few minutes. He was connected to the machine through a series of wires attached to his chest. He wore a cap with at least a dozen wires coming out of it. Those wires were all connected to another machine, but at least that one didn't beep. It was monitored by the special doctor outside the window.

How could anyone possibly sleep like this?

The cap shifted a little as Adam turned his head to look through the window into the other room. There were no lights on in Adam's room, but the light from the other room came through the window and provided a night light for him. His mom and dad sat in there with the doctor and Ms. Brown from his school. His mom promised to stay the whole time. She always kept her promises. Sometimes his dad forgot what he promised, but Adam usually forgave him.

Adam looked at the tall doctor standing with them. He had flown in special just to see Adam. Adam couldn't imagine why he was so special that the doctor came all the way from Washington D.C. just to help him stop having nightmares and wetting the bed.

Adam sighed and turned his head to look at the ceiling again.

This is so embarrassing. They'd better not tell anyone.
And it better work.

His eyes started to feel heavy from the medication the doctor gave him. He said it was a "light sedative." He said a long name that Adam's dad recognized but nobody else did. They all just smiled and told Adam everything was going to be okay. Adam's dad was the only one who didn't seem to think this was going to be some miracle. Adam could tell his dad thought the whole thing was stupid.

It probably is stupid. I'll just go to sleep and get it over with.

He closed his eyes and let himself relax.

"Yes, go to sleep."

Adam's eyes flew open. He rolled his head around and looked for who else was in the room but saw no one. Did he imagine it?

He turned and looked through the window. His mom and dad were still there, his dad looking annoyed. The doctor looked at his computer screen. Ms. Brown stared through the glass and played with her hair. Adam turned his head slightly to see what she was looking at, but there was nothing there. She was staring awfully hard at nothing.

There's nothing there, Susan told herself. *It's a reflection of light on the glass.*

A chill in Susan's spine contradicted her thoughts as a familiar essence scented the air.

Peppermint.

She closed her eyes, in an attempt to blink away what she saw.

She had blonde hair. She always wanted red hair like mine.

Susan opened her eyes. The image was still there, though faint, just at the foot of the bed. A girl with blonde hair and a pink nightgown.

Susan stood motionless, too afraid to make the slightest movement or sound as her fingers stopped twisting in her hair, her eyes stayed open, wide, and unable to blink, her mouth gapped just the slightest bit, the breath stayed stuck in her lungs, and her heart raced with the adrenaline of fear, pushing racing blood through her body up to her ears where it beat against her eardrums with a raging pulse.

Then many things happened very quickly:

Adam screamed.

The girl turned and looked directly at Susan.

Susan gasped and stumbled back.

Amanda stood up too fast and crashed into Susan as she stumbled.

The girl disappeared.

Susan dropped the lock of hair she had pulled from her head.

The peppermint was gone.

It was three hours later when Adam was back in his own bed and his parents lay talking quietly in theirs. Thomas had his arm around his wife as she laid on her side and cried into her pillow.

"I feel terrible. Have I scarred him for life?"

"Adam will be fine. He just got scared," Thomas reassured her, though he was pretty sure they would be paying for therapy in a few years.

Weeks, more like it.

"But, *why* did he get scared?"

Thomas didn't know the answer. The sound of his son's blood-curdling scream seemed to still ring in his ears. It wasn't just a normal fear of the doctor. Thomas had seen that plenty of times. This was different. Deeper.

Adam peeked over the edge of his blanket at the foot of the bed. He saw his dresser with his three model cars sitting on top like they always did. A movie poster with a team of brightly costumed superheroes who appeared ready for a fight hung on the wall. A mismatched collection of toy cars lay strewn about the room, along with at least a few days' worth of dirty clothes. Adam knew his mom was worried when she brought him into the room because she didn't mention the mess like she normally did.

Aside from his mom's lack of nagging, everything seemed to be just as it should be. But something still tensed inside Adam, an unease that clung to his belly and tightened his chest. He was afraid if he closed his eyes, something that shouldn't be in his room would come in anyway, like it did at the sleep study.

He didn't know what it was, but something had been there.

Adam crossed himself the way he was taught at church school, the way his parents always did before they prayed.

"Father, Son, and Holy Ghost," he whispered almost silently.

Forehead, chest, left shoulder, right. Or was it right shoulder, left? Sometimes he couldn't remember. He crossed himself both ways, so he knew he was covered.

"Father, Son, and Holy Ghost," he whispered again.

The last word caught in his throat as he said it.

Ghost.

It couldn't have been. Adam didn't believe in ghosts. They were the things of dumb movies made to scare people. He had been scared a few times, too. His parents told him there was no such thing as ghosts. He believed them. Why shouldn't he?

But he heard the voice. The voice from nobody. It came from nothing.

The Nothing.

The thought surprised Adam. It came into his mind almost like a thought bubble in a comic book. Like someone else wrote it right there in his brain. He didn't know what it was, but it frightened him more than any pretend movie ever did, this nothing.

The Nothing.

Adam pulled the blanket back over his head and squeezed his eyes shut.

Miles away, Susan sat at her dining table and watched the flame of the match as she lit another cigarette. It was a bad habit she slipped into when she was stressed, and boy, was she stressed. The smoke tasted stale on her tongue, then stung and burned her throat as she inhaled a deep, pleasing hit. Her lungs rejected it with a cough like they always did on her first smoke after a long period of abstinence. Normally, she would chastise herself for falling off the smoke-free wagon. Tonight was different.

She didn't go in to see Adam after he got scared and screamed. She was too afraid herself to go into that room. That, she did chastise herself over. Still, it wasn't her place to soothe him. His parents were there for that. They were the people he trusted and who had cared for him and protected him for all eight years of his life.

The first time it was up to her to protect him, she froze.

Who could blame her? She thought she saw a ghost. The ghost of her long-dead sister, no less.

Which was ridiculous.

Leave it to the therapist to be so screwed up in the head.

She gave a silent dry laugh, then sucked hard on her cigarette again.

But I'm not really a therapist. I'm a research psychologist, she reminded herself. *This is just my role in the research.*

And what was Adam's role?

She knew what it was. For the first time, she didn't know if she had it in her to go through with the plan.

The tip of the cigarette glowed red as she inhaled deeply once again. There was no cough this time and she held the smoke in her lungs for several seconds before slowly releasing the trapped breath. She watched it linger in the air in front of her, turning and taking on shapes in the slight breeze that came through the nearby open window, before it faded and disappeared.

Just like Sarah.

Susan shook her head against the thought. It was some trick of the memory, what she saw a few hours ago. Her sister had been gone for nearly 30 years. She had nothing to do with what she and Jackson were doing now. Still, Susan's hand shook as she put the cigarette to her lips once again. It was burned down nearly to the filter and the hot smoke entered her throat like fire itself, flames tearing at flesh like barbed wire as she swallowed it down. She sputtered and gasped as her lungs rejected its poison and the smoke, cool now, fought its way back up and out into the air as she coughed hard and tried in gulps to catch her breath, eyes watering to the point of tears and head throbbing with every painful expulsion.

Then, a flash of gold.

Just in the far-right reach of her vision.

Not gold.

Blonde.

Susan's breath stopped. She dropped the cigarette on the table, missing the ashtray by an inch, and frantically blinked away the wetness from her eyes. Her heart raced but the rest of her refused to move, like a scared animal hoping its stillness would hide it from a looming predator. Her breath came back in short, silent bursts that felt nearly as fast as her heartbeat. She sat, paralyzed by fear, for a long moment as the cigarette burned itself out on the table.

"It was nothing," she said out loud. "There's nothing there."

Great, now I'm seeing things and *talking to myself.*

She put the cigarette butt in the ashtray and used her fingertip to try to smudge out the slight burn mark it left on the table before getting up and going to bed.

She never noticed the slight scent of peppermint mixed with the odor of her cigarette.

Chapter 4

"What happens to us when we die? Would you say that is one of the most asked questions around the world, in any nation, in any time period?" Jackson watched himself in a full-length mirror. "What about when we sleep? What happens to us then?"

He was rehearsing for his next speech which was to be given on Wednesday. It was Monday now. He'd taken a red-eye flight home Saturday night after the failed experiment in San Francisco and spent Sunday working in his office organizing data from his recent studies.

"They're both questions of consciousness, sleeping and dying. Where does the consciousness go when the mind isn't aware of it? Just think about that for a minute, but from a scientific perspective. I'm not talking about metaphysics here. It's the question of life after death, being answered by *science*. The answer is right there," he plucked at the air in front of him "but we haven't found a way to grasp it. That is what I'm working on. I'm studying the boundaries of consciousness–no, the *capabilities* of consciousness–which will lead us to discover what consciousness can do without the limits of the mind and body. That is the *true* life after death."

Jackson gave a pleased smile to his reflection. His speech was perfect, with just the right amount of drama to keep the weaker minds listening. He always rehearsed in front of the mirror in his bedroom so he could perfect his movements and facial expressions. His mother started him on it when he was very young. He never seemed to have the right expression, or any expression at all for that matter. She taught him to how to show happiness and excitement, and kindness and love. He learned anger, resentment, and indifference from his father.

He picked his speech notes up off the bed and took them with him to his home office where he placed them in a neat stack on the top of a handsome and organized desk. He sat down at it and pulled another stack of papers from one of the desk drawers. They were tinged yellow with age, though they were now in protective holders made of clear plastic. It was a collection of fifty or so pages, many handwritten and the rest bearing the slightly staggered and uneven print of an electric typewriter. The typist was unskilled, given the number of corrections done on each page.

Jackson had thumbed through these notes at least monthly for ten years. He had them memorized. They were original notes of research from the 1980s, conducted by a Dr. Smith. Jackson assumed it wasn't his real name, given the controversial nature of the research and the clandestine way in which he became the owner of the notes. One day, someone simply left them on his desk at work. No one knew where they came from, or no one admitted to it.

The research studied the psychic abilities of children. That in itself wasn't too controversial, though it was often disregarded as pseudoscience. The problem was that the researcher's methods weren't always what would be considered ethical. The children often didn't have parental supervision, they were forced to participate in things that frightened them, and one of the children died. That's when the research, and the notes, ended.

That's where Jackson started.

His own research was built around what the other researcher discovered, though he planned to never tell anyone that.

San Francisco

Adam didn't want to go to school, but he also didn't want to make his parents more worried about him. His mom treated him like a baby all day Sunday, and he didn't want to stay home and do that again. So he went to school, but he crossed his fingers that he wouldn't have to see Ms. Brown today. He liked Ms. Brown, but the whole experience Saturday night had been humiliating.

He was disappointed to learn that crossing one's fingers doesn't always work. At least she asked him to come during math. Adam knew she did that on purpose for him, and as he walked to her office he decided that made it better.

"Good morning, Adam. Why don't you shut the door?" Her greeting worried him. Grownups only wanted the door closed when it was something bad. He shut the door and sat down in the chair across from her desk.

"Good morning, Ms. Brown," he said once he was settled. He held his favorite toy car in his hands—a bright red Ford Mustang. He was allowed to have it with him in here.

"Adam, I want to apologize to you. That study Saturday night wasn't intended to stress you like that, and I'm sorry that it did," she said.

He thought he should say something, but no words came to mind. On top of that, his throat felt swollen with a lump that suddenly appeared. His face felt hot, and his eyes threatened to tear up if he looked away from the car he twirled over and over in his hands. He kept his head down.

Ms. Brown folded her hands on her desk. "It's okay if you're mad at me for suggesting that to your parents."

"I'm not mad," Adam said, his voice just above a whisper. "I just don't know why I got scared like that."

"Sometimes fear happens for no reason. It's okay."

"Do you ever get scared for no reason?"

"Yes, I do," Ms. Brown said. She leaned onto the desk just a little and whispered. "In fact, I scared myself later that very night and went to bed with every light in the house turned on."

Adam looked up at her and smiled. "Really?"

"Yes, really."

Adam thought it over. Grownups get scared, too, and even sleep with the lights on sometimes. What could be so bad that an adult would be that scared? He didn't want to know. Still, he felt better now. He felt so good, he was able to get back to class in time to take a math test, and he didn't even mind.

He agreed to see Ms. Brown again on Friday. On Fridays he got dropped off fifteen minutes early, so Ms. Brown said she'd come in early and meet with him then. He was looking forward to it.

Susan waited a few minutes to make sure Adam wouldn't come back in, then dug her cell phone out of her purse, typed a single word into a text, and sent it.

Friday.

That was all that was needed. The plan was in motion.

She sat silently and twirled a lock of hair between her fingers.

Chapter 5

Friday

Thomas balanced on the edge of hysteria. His wife was already there. When their son didn't get off the bus after school, they discovered he never made it to his class that morning. By now, he had been missing for twelve hours. Panic swelled inside Thomas. He wanted to be strong for his wife, to help her through this moment, but the terror rose inside him and made it impossible. Together, they had searched the neighborhood, paced the floor, found dozens of pictures for the police, and called everyone they could think of. Neighbors were now out with flashlights canvassing the area. Even from inside their home, they heard the occasional shout of their son's name. "Adam! Adam Hernandez, are you out there?"

Thomas now sat in the dark on the edge of Adam's bed. He counted off the rosary beads between his fingers as he begged the Virgin Mary and Saint Joseph for the safety of his son. Deep in prayer, he startled at the touch of a hand on his shoulder. Light streamed in from the open bedroom door as his own father sat down on the bed beside him.

"What can we do?" the elder asked.

"Find my boy."

"We will." Gabriel Hernandez placed an arm around his son. Even a grown man who was always the protector of others sometimes needed a person who was strong just for him.

Thomas surrendered to it as the panic flooded out in the form of tears. He was grateful beyond words for his father's presence in the room. As he had done so many times throughout Thomas's life, his father gave him hope while also allowing him the freedom to go through his emotions. Gabriel wasn't Thomas's biological father, but that had never mattered. He was a good man who fell in love with a woman who happened to be pregnant. She had been seduced by a sweet-talking older man who quickly disappeared. She never said anything more than that. They were married before Thomas was born, and Gabriel was his father every moment after.

At this moment, Thomas was surprised to realize how much he needed it.

Thomas was always good at handling stressful situations. He was the one who found the answers and created a plan of action. Those qualities were why he was such a good emergency room doctor. As a doctor, he lacked a little in his bedside manner but not because he didn't care. He was always focused on the immediate problem, and that often led to rushed directness. He consciously tried to work on that, and on a problem he had with his temper.

He rarely lost his temper in person, and never at work, but he recognized that his fuse was pretty short at times. He was always careful about it and didn't want anyone to ever see him angry. Even his wife had never seen his full temper. They rarely disagreed, and on the odd occasion when they did, his temper never flared up. He kept it in check with his prayers and daily Mass. He prayed that God would take it from him, and usually, God answered that prayer.

Now, in the panic of his son's disappearance, he could feel that temper burning somewhere deep inside him. It was smothered in fear and worry, but it was in there.

He wasn't sure what would happen if it broke out.

Burley, Idaho

Adam felt the back-and-forth swaying of movement and heard the rattle of cupboard doors that weren't closed tight enough.

Am I on a boat? That didn't seem right, but his mind was fuzzy, and it took a moment for his thoughts to clear. He knew he was laying on his side on something soft, but he was moving. He kept his eyes pressed closed and listened to the sounds around him. Memories came back slowly. A woman, nice and pretty, like his mom. After that, everything went fuzzy again.

He slowly opened his eyes just enough to see some light through his eyelashes. A sharp pain pierced through his skull, his stomach lurched and he was afraid he would throw up. He wished the swaying would stop. He needed help.

"Mom?" It came out in a whispered plea but as soon as he said it, he wished he hadn't. He didn't know who was there, but he was certain his mother wasn't. He closed his eyes even tighter to hold his tears inside. He laid curled up with his eyes clamped shut and a hand over his face as he felt the swaying slowly come to a rest. His stomach turned as he heard someone quietly coming close.

"Adam?" Her voice was gentle, but it wasn't his mother. He felt her get closer to him and rest her hand softly on his head. "Does it hurt?"

He slowly nodded.

"I'm going to give you something to make it stop hurting. It's a little injection, but I promise you it'll make the pain go away fast."

Adam's body tensed at the thought of getting a shot.

"Are you a doctor?" he asked.

"I am. This needle is very small. You'll hardly feel it." The woman's voice was quiet and comforting. He started to recognize it. Adam flinched at the prick of the needle, but it wasn't as bad as he expected. "There, in a few minutes, your head will feel better."

"Am I in the hospital?"

"No, you are on an adventure."

"Why does my head hurt?"

"I had to give you something to make you fall asleep. Do you remember? It sometimes makes you wake up with a headache, but I was prepared for that." She stroked his hair like his mother did when he was sick. "Don't worry about a thing. I'm going to make sure you're okay."

As the pain faded, his thoughts cleared. Adam did remember. She asked him to help her carry something to her car down the block. When they got there, she walked up behind him and grabbed his arm. He felt a pinch, and that's when things got fuzzy. He remembered waking up a little bit as she carried him and laid him down on this couch. His thoughts stopped and he drew in a fast, loud breath as he finally realized what happened.

"Ms. Brown?"

The woman's hand stopped moving. Her voice sounded weak. "You just be good, and everything will be fine. I'm going to make sure you're okay."

Adam pressed his back into the cushion behind him. It was all he could do to put more inches between them.

"Did you take me? Are you taking me?"

His heart pounded so hard in his chest, that Adam was sure it would pound its way out. He wanted to yell or run and jump out the door, but the same fear that made his legs long to run also made them completely useless. He knew he was never going to see his mom and dad again. Fear and loneliness smothered him and hollowed him out at the same time. Even if he got away, would his parents still want him after he had done something so stupid? They always told him never to talk to strangers and absolutely never go off with one. But Ms. Brown wasn't a stranger. She worked at his school. She was his friend.

And now here he was, the stupidest boy in the world, scared of the dark, alone with a lying kidnapper, and missing his parents so much he couldn't bear the feeling of it.

He ached with the terror and grief that gripped him so strongly, that the only thing he could do to protect himself from the feeling was to fall back to sleep.

Rural Minnesota

"Where are you?"

"I don't know."

"Where am I?"

"You're home, asleep in your bed. You know that."

He was right. Aurea knew she was safe at home, asleep in her bed. But she was also here, in a cold, damp meadow with the little boy.

"You have to find me," the boy pleaded.

"If this is a dream, why do I know that I'm dreaming?" she asked him. He didn't answer. The space around her turned dark and empty. The boy cried as he faded into the emptiness. Aurea reached out, desperate to grasp him, but at her touch, he dissolved into smoke and blew away.

She was alone in the darkness.

It was cold on her skin and seeped a chill into her bones like a wet winter day. She turned her head and searched for light, just a pinprick of a glow to give her some bearings. There was nothing. Even the air was empty. Her lungs burned for oxygen, but there was none. She turned again, looking for a place to run, or any possible way out of the dark. All she saw was an eternity of black. Despair blanketed her.

It was as if the despair formed into a mass, a living being there in the darkness with her. It was alive and it wanted to feed on her. The liquid stench of it, like death and rot, seeped into her nose and stung her eyes. It pressed against her lips as it tried to invade her. Dark tentacles, even darker than the blackness that surrounded her, reached for her and circled scaled, wet limbs around her legs, her arms, her throat. It strangled her and she gasped for air. Instead, it was water as cold as ice that filled her lungs, setting them strangely afire, as the tentacles held tight and pulled her down.

Aurea jolted upright in the bed and grabbed her throat as she was startled awake. She took in deep gulps of air and could still feel the grip the monster had on her. To her left, something slithered along the wall, a dark blur of a shadow. She whipped her head around to look for it, but there was nothing there. Was it her imagination? The dream, the moving shadow, it was so real, she looked around the room to make sure the beast wasn't in there with her. She jumped again with the sudden ringing of her cellphone and had to catch her breath before answering. It was rare for her to get phone calls, especially this time of night.

"Hello?" She expected it to be a wrong number or one of the hundreds of scam calls going around.

"There's a child who needs you." It was a woman's voice on the other end.

"Excuse me?"

"You have a choice right now. You can hang up and pretend this call didn't happen, or you can get up, get dressed, and do what I tell you. Which do you choose?"

"Who is this?"

"I work with Jackson."

Aurea froze at the mention of his name. She was confused, but she now knew this wasn't some random scammer or prank call.

Irritation rose in the woman's voice. "I don't have much time for this. Are you listening?"

"Yes."

"Check your frequent flier account. You'll find that you have a new reservation. You leave in three hours. That should just give you enough time to get to the airport," she said. "I can't imagine why someone would live so far from a city."

"How did you get into my miles account?" Aurea tried to make sense of what the woman was saying. "How do you have my phone number?"

"We have a lot of information on you. Jackson is very good at research," the caller said. "Get on the plane. When you land, I'll text you where to go. The little boy is counting on you."

"Adam?"

"You're very connected to him, aren't you? Why could that be?" Her tone held sarcasm. "The connection runs deep in your family. It would be good for you to remember that now."

Without more explanation, the call ended. Aurea paused for only a moment before accessing her frequent flier account on her phone. She had a ticket to San Francisco and a growing sense of dread. Mostly, she was overwhelmed with fear for the boy. She was not the right person to save anyone's life.

Reagan National Airport, Arlington, Virginia

Nerves seldom rattled Jackson. He was a careful man who planned with tedious attention to detail. Still, there were times it eased his mind to talk to his only trusted confidant. This was one of them. He found a secluded corner in the airport to make a private phone call while he awaited his flight. He dialed and waited for her to answer.

"Well, hello. Are you getting ready to board?" she asked.

"The flight is delayed. How are things there?"

"Quiet, now. Are you alright? It's not like you to call this late."

"I'm fine. I thought we should run through a few details as we prepare to get the study underway." Jackson kept his tone professional. It was how he operated best. "This is the same as any other scientific experiment. I've spent the last ten years researching and observing what select people can do with their minds, and how they seem to know things without explanation. I've found evidence that some can pull thoughts and ideas from other people."

He paused and thought about what he had accomplished. Over many months, he carefully constructed his hypothesis about the reality of a common consciousness and the ability to manipulate it. He then spent years conducting experiments and research at the lab under the guise of learning more about the function of the human brain. It was exhilarating.

"It's very exciting work, Jackson. How did it go with the last boy you saw?"

"He continues to show progress. I believe with a little more focus, he'll soon be able to see both images simultaneously," Jackson said. "But it's the girls I was thinking of just now."

"Tell me about them again."

Jackson pushed down his irritation. She knew this information. She had listened to him read the notes out loud time and time again. Still, she was the only person who knew as much about it as he did, and it was good to have someone to listen to him.

"It's an experiment that was conducted regularly over two years with two gifted subjects. Two young sisters tried to send images of toys to one another as the doctor monitored their brain waves," he explained. "He had seen the children more than sixty times over the two years, and they showed great potential. They were just three and five years old when the experiments started. So young, with very open minds."

He explained that the doctor placed the girls in separate observation rooms and gave each a box of toys. The first girl would choose a toy, focus on it, and send the thought to her sister. The other girl was to retrieve the thought, then find in her box the toy her sister had selected.

"For the first several visits, the results were equal with a child guessing which toy to choose. Once the doctor started introducing more stimulus and higher stakes, the results started to change," he said. "He traded out the toys for pictures to eliminate the possibility of the girls planning ahead which toys would be chosen. He also changed out the pictures each time so they couldn't be memorized. One girl would focus on the picture, and the girl in the other room would try to draw it."

"That was very smart," she said.

"The doctor rotated different types of stimuli to see what was the most effective," he continued. "Some weeks he promised the reward of ice cream. Others, he made the rooms uncomfortably cold and would turn up the heat with each correct drawing,"

Those were the experiments he would share when he published his research. Other things, he would keep to himself. Such as letting one sister believe the other would be hurt if the experiment didn't work or making them sit in the dark while playing frightening sounds over an intercom. The girls' mother had signed a confidentiality agreement and the doctor paid the woman handsomely for their time, always in cash. Jackson suspected the doctor kept his conscience clear by never physically hurting the girls, and they always got candy at the end of the session. That's what all good doctors did.

One of the last experiments had once again confirmed that fear was the strongest incentive. When the girls were afraid, either for themselves or for the other sister, their results were the strongest. Jackson had seen it himself in several of his own experiments, both with the children and the adults he studied.

"Through the doctor's notes, I was able to ascertain which stimuli lead to the greatest improvements in brain activity. He found that the girls' ability to transmit thoughts to each other increased with the right incentives." Jackson smiled. "It is truly groundbreaking, a look into the collective consciousness."

He felt better as they ended the call a few moments later.

The transmission of thoughts was just part of his research. The other part focused on discovering how it worked. He explained it only once publicly at one of his fundraisers.

"A recent theory centered on the idea of two types of brainwaves, the electromagnetic brainwaves and another type of wave that was much more difficult to define: mass in energy form," he told the crowd. "Scientists have discovered the duality of atoms. They can exist in particle form or wave form. Atoms make up everything. Everything you see or touch or ever come into contact with is made up of atoms. These atoms can move from particle form to wave form.

Think of particles as mass or something we can touch. Waves are like radio waves that we can't touch but are still there."

"Since we know that these atoms can change from particle form to wave form, then we can deduce that there is a type of wave made up of atoms," he continued. "These waves are atoms in energy form. Mass in energy form."

Jackson's excitement built and he paced the front of the stage.

"Something that we once could touch, now in energy form. These are the second brainwaves we scientists are learning about," he said, his voice breathy with exhilaration. "Keeping in mind that energy is limitless, these brainwaves are the energy that connects us to everything in the universe."

There it was: Everything he worked so hard to prove, all in one sentence. His chest rose and fell with each breath as he gazed out at the audience and anticipated their understanding.

It didn't come.

The speech was met with lukewarm applause as the audience took the time to work out what he explained. Still, as he remembered it now in the airport, he was proud of his presentation. He wanted people to understand what he was working so hard to prove.

Now, he was ready for a much more dramatic study.

He spent time making sure he selected the right test subjects. He learned as much as he could about Aurea, although the past few years of her life were pretty uneventful. He already knew about her mother's supposed talents in mysticism. While Jackson dismissed any divine reasoning for it, he did believe she was accessing the force of consciousness that he sought. It was too bad she died before this study. She would have made a fantastic subject. Still, her daughter would be nearly just as good, especially when given the right motivation, he thought.

The choice to bring Adam into the study came about through a fortunate discovery. As Jackson was studying Aurea, he discovered that she, too, was studying someone – their half-brother who lived in San Francisco. Jackson wasn't surprised at the discovery. He knew about his father's earlier habits with women. He was, however, disgusted by it. There was more of his father's seed in the world. Even worse, the man had a son. Jackson spent months researching his siblings, flying around the nation to watch them, and getting into their personal records. Some would call it stalking. To him, it was simply part of the scientific process. His study wouldn't be accurate unless he knew everything about the people involved. The more he learned, the more intrigued he became. He even discovered secrets he was sure other people didn't know, especially about Adam.

Adam was the perfect catalyst for his siblings' abilities. He was also the last of his father's bloodline and his death would end Jack Cole's existence in the world. That was the only part of the study that evoked emotion in Jackson. The rest was purely his quest for understanding, and to let the world know Jackson Cole was the one who made the biggest scientific discovery that humans will ever understand.

His final experiment pulled together his research. He would monitor the boy's brainwaves with a small electroencephalogram device. It was worn like a hat and was typically used to help people who suffer from seizures. He had worked out a way to make the boy keep it on his head. He would then put the child in an impossible situation filled with stimuli and document the results. Could the boy send out his atom brainwaves and lead his rescuer to him? Jackson believed he could. He believed the study would show that not only do these quantum brainwaves exist but that humans have the potential to learn to direct the waves to anywhere in the universe.

Proof of quantum consciousness. It would change humanity.

And Jackson Cole would be the most revered person on Earth.

Chapter 6

"Excuse me, Thomas?"

The woman's voice startled him. Thomas was kneeling in prayer, saying the same prayer he'd been saying since they discovered Adam's disappearance more than 12 hours ago. He came to the cathedral this morning with the hope that maybe if he said the prayer in church, God would hear it more clearly. Part of him thought that was ridiculous, but another part was willing to do anything. He looked up at the woman who had interrupted him.

"We've never met, but I know you're suffering a great deal right now. I want to help."

Thomas didn't have the strength at this moment to talk to another kind stranger who wanted to help. He appreciated it, but he had nothing left in him this morning.

"We have a search party organized. I can give you the number for the police officer in charge," he told her as he sat back into the pew. He wanted to be irritated when the woman slid into the pew next to him, but she looked at him with such gentleness and understanding, he felt his resolve soften. She took one of his hands in both of hers, a gesture that somehow lessened the anxiety that choked him.

"Thomas, I'm here to help you get Adam back. In order to do that, I need to tell you some things that you may not like." The woman took a deep breath. "And frankly, you may think I'm a little nuts."

"Do you know something? Where is my son?"

"I don't know where he is, but I know who took him."

Thomas's body trembled with worry and anger. His voice was low and commanding, a tone that was a surprise even to Thomas. "Tell me how to find my son."

"Thomas, my name is Aurea. I'm your sister." She paused as if awaiting a reaction from Thomas. He didn't give her one. "Your half-sister. You and I share a father. There's another of us, our half-brother. I believe he's the one who took Adam."

Thomas was silent, then shook his head. Whether in disagreement or to shake some sense into it, he didn't know.

"That's not possible. I don't understand."

"Thomas, what do you know about your biological father?"

"Nothing." It was the plain truth. Thomas never had any information about the man. He had tried once, but the search didn't take him very far.

"I found out who my father was several years ago and started doing research. That's how I found out you were my brother. You did a genealogy test. When I did mine, I marked that I didn't want my information given out. They weren't allowed to tell you about me, but I knew about you. I just never wanted to interrupt your life."

"What does this have to do with my son?" Thomas counted methodically to four as he drew in a deep breath, then counted again as he slowly released it. It was a habit he slipped into without thinking anytime he started to feel overwhelmed. It also helped him control his temper.

"Thomas, our father was a man from back east who came to California often during the 80s. He met your mother here in San Francisco and my mother down the coast. He already had a wife and a child at home, and a blossoming career, so it makes sense that he wanted everything about you and me kept quiet."

Thomas needed time to process the information, but the woman continued.

"That man became a very well-known doctor and that other son he had is a pretty well-known scientist."

"Who?" Thomas paused for an answer and noticed Aurea take a deep breath.

"Doctor Jack Cole. His other son is the scientist, Doctor Jackson Cole."

It took him no time to recognize the name, and instantly it felt like his stomach hit the floor. He tried to force his body to breathe. It wasn't possible. It simply wasn't possible.

This woman must have heard about that damn sleep study and now wants to get something from me.

His face flushed with heat and his hands balled up into fists as he stood up too quickly and knocked into the pew in front of him. He wanted to pick it up and throw it, like he wanted to physically throw the woman out of the church. He glared at her through tense eyelids for only a second before turning and heading for the door. He saw nothing but what was directly in front of him and his ears stopped hearing anything with detail. He was already in the parking lot and near his car when his hearing started to become normal again and his vision expanded out of the tunnel created by the sudden, intense anger. He slowed down and steadied his breathing, then realized the woman was chasing behind him. He turned around and nearly stepped into her as accusations tumbled out of him.

"Are you a lunatic? Is this what you do, go to church and prey on people whose children are missing? Are you looking for money? Do you just like to hurt people? What game are you playing?"

Thomas turned back around and headed for his car. His hands were shaking so badly from the adrenaline, he couldn't get his keys out of his pocket. Fury threatened to again make his vision narrow and his mind dizzy. He turned, leaned his back against the car, and closed his eyes. He wasn't sure why he was suddenly so angry. So what if his father now had a name? But that wasn't it. This woman was saying that Thomas's mother had an affair with a married man, and that wasn't possible. On top of that, she's claiming this famous scientist half-brother has kidnapped the person Thomas loved most in the world. What was this woman after?

He opened his eyes and stared at her. He wanted to get a good look at the woman so he could give the police a description when he told them what happened.

She hadn't moved since he stormed off. She looked hurt, but calm. As he watched, the San Francisco wind picked up and blew her long hair around her face. He noticed then that she had an unusual hairline that came to a slight point in the middle above her eyes. A widow's peak, it was called. It's a rare hereditary feature. Thomas had one. Adam was bald as a newborn, but when his hair grew in, Thomas was touched to see that Adam had one as well. Thomas then researched it and found only about 35 percent of all people had a widow's peak.

He pulled out his phone and did an image search for Jackson Cole. The first image was the man and his father.

They both had the same rare hairline.

Thomas's legs gave out and he sank hard to the ground. Aurea was quickly at his side.

"I saw a bench in the garden over there. Let's go talk," she said.

A few moments later, Thomas sat with his phone in his hands. Aurea sat next to him. He had just called Jackson Cole's Washington, D.C. office and left a message with an assistant. He wasn't sure what he would say if someone called him back.

"I want to explain this to you, but I need you to try to have an open mind for a moment," she said to him. "You're a devout Catholic?"

"I am."

"So, you believe in angels and saints, and that they can give you help and guidance?"

"Yes, of course. What are you getting at?"

"I believe the same thing; I was just raised calling it something different. I can go deep in prayer and ask for insight into situations in my life. You have a strong connection to your saints and angels, so you can understand that I have a strong connection to mine."

"Sure," Thomas shrugged. "Are you saying angels told you this guy kidnapped my son?"

"I'm saying years ago, I formed a connection with our half-brother. Not a pleasant one, but still a connection. I've been aware of him—and you—for most of my life. And I guess he's been aware of me." Aurea shuddered at the realization. "Last night, I got a phone call from a woman who told me I had to help Adam. She even had a plane ticket for me to fly out here."

"Who was she? Call her back."

"I don't know. Thomas, just follow with me a little bit more, and then we will go to the police. Before we go, you need to understand more about Jackson."

"You have three minutes. I've already been gone too long."

"Okay. You have your saints and angels. I have my beliefs. Jackson has *science*. He studied quantum physics and now works for a foundation that's trying to solve all these mysteries about the human mind. I've studied it only a little, to try to learn some of what he knows. It's the scientific study of how everything in existence is connected. There are many paths that this takes. The one Jackson followed deals with consciousness. Just like you connect with your religion, and I connect with mine, Jackson thinks that through this science he can connect with anything he wants."

"What does this have to do with Adam?"

Aurea lowered her gaze. "I don't know exactly."

"Then why are you wasting my time? This is crazy. Why-" Thomas was cut off by the ringing of his cell phone. No number showed up on the caller ID. He opened an app on his phone and then connected the call. "Hello?"

"It seems our sister has found you."

Surprise took Thomas's words. He looked at Aurea. *Who the hell are these people?*

"Who is this? Where is my son?"

"You called me, Thomas. You left your number with my office. And as you know, we've already met."

Thomas struggled to believe what he was hearing. His voice was weak under the crushing flurry of emotions. "Where is Adam?"

"He's very gifted, you know. He sees Aurea in his dreams. He thinks she's his guardian angel. Did she tell you that? No? Regardless, he makes for a very interesting subject." Thomas heard intrigue in Jackson's voice. "I think it's an opportunity for a fascinating case study. Yes, you tell the police who has your son and everyone in the U.S. will be looking for us. But, trust me, no one will find us. It will be up to Adam. He can tell Aurea where to find him, and if you two find him in time, you'll bring your son home with you."

"How much time do we have?"

"That depends. How long can your son survive without you?" Jackson's voice took on a firm tone, "The parameters are set. The police, the Secret Service, the FBI, the media, and every soccer mom in America can search in the normal ways. But none of them talk to you or Aurea after twelve this afternoon. You two search on your own. And if you cheat, the game's over."

Thomas stared at the phone as the call ended. He stopped the recording app he had started before answering and checked to see if it recorded properly. He then looked over at the woman he had known for only twenty minutes. She was now his son's lifeline.

"Officers are waiting with my wife at our house. We need to get there fast."

Near Billings, Montana

"There's no going back now." Jackson pocketed his phone and looked at his assistant. The woman rushed as she packed a cardboard box with food from the pantry. She had already packed two other boxes with towels and things from around the cabin. "Why are you packing so much?"

"Every time we stop for food, we risk someone recognizing us," she said as she dropped a can of beans into the box. She stopped and looked at him. "Would you turn back if you could?"

"No." Jackson didn't hesitate. "Once this is done, everyone will understand what I did. What *we* did."

He would be a legend, and he would achieve his lifelong goal of destroying his father.

Jackson looked at his watch. It was just after 10:30 a.m. Mountain Time, which made it 9:30 in California. Two and a half hours until his study started, but he only had minutes until the authorities were notified. It would take some time for them to verify that it was he who was involved, but once they did, his life would forever be different.

"Have you packed everything you need?" Susan asked him. "Adam will be awake again soon."

They had used allergy medication to lull the boy to sleep this time. Susan didn't want to give him any more shots.

"Yes. My laptop, notebooks, and briefcase are already in the motorhome."

"Did you pack clothes?"

"Susan, I'm not the one you're supposed to be mothering," he said. Susan was a good researcher, good enough to commit a major federal crime in the name of science, but Jackson did not like to be nagged. He reminded himself that Susan believed he had romantic feelings for her and coaxed his expression into the soft smile he used when he needed to appear gentle. "But you're right. I still need to pack my bag."

He hurried down the hall to his room and took a duffle bag out of the closet. He normally visited his cabin a few times a year when he needed solitude. He kept plenty of clothes and supplies there so he wouldn't have to bring luggage with him when he visited. He filled the duffle with clothes and checked his watch. It was time to get on the road.

He wasn't too worried about what would happen to him if he got caught. His family's influence and money had a way of making even tough situations disappear. His concern was about the experiment. It had come too far to be stopped. He wouldn't allow it.

"As we discussed, I will soon be tracked to this cabin," Jackson said as he walked back into the kitchen. "By now, the authorities in San Francisco have been notified. I'm certain they will take their next steps with caution, and so will we."

Jackson took his cell phone out of his pocket and placed it on the kitchen table. He looked around one last time to make sure he had everything.

"I'll get the boxes. You get the kid, and we'll be on the road," he said, "It's about time the Coles had a family reunion."

Adam

The cold always came first.

First, he knew he was cold. Then, he knew he was afraid.

Afraid of what?

Adam didn't know. He couldn't see anything.

"Hello," he called out. There was no answer.

Adam turned his head but everywhere he looked there was only emptiness.

Somehow, Adam knew what came next: a sickly-sweet scent, then just a little bit of light. Then, a girl. She was about his age, with blonde hair and a pink nightgown. The old-fashioned kind, with a cartoon bear on it like something his mom would have worn when she was a kid.

But this wasn't a childhood image of his mother. The girl moved closer to him, and he saw her face was pale. Even her lips were nearly white. He watched those bloodless lips as she spoke.

"You going to come keep me company. I'm bringing you to me."

"No!" Adam screamed. He turned to run from her, but everywhere he turned, she was there.

"I just want someone to play with," she told him as she reached out to grab him.

On the other nights, this is when Adam awoke. His sheets would be wet and he would be embarrassed that he had been so scared and stuck in his nightmare that he didn't wake up and make it to the bathroom like a normal kid. The dream never let him out in time.

This time, her touch didn't wake him. She gripped both his arms with hard, cold fingers that were much too strong for a child.

"You're the only one who will come with me," she said to him. "Don't leave me alone here."

Adam tried to twist away from her grip. It was getting even colder and darker in this Nothing place and his panic swelled. The girl just held tighter.

"Even if you leave now, I'm bringing you to me," she said.

Adam stopped moving and closed his eyes. "I have to wake up."

As soon as the thought formed, Adam's eyes fluttered, and the nightmare faded. He didn't recognize the room he was in, but he knew he was awake. He was relieved to discover that he was also dry.

His head was fuzzy again, but at least it didn't hurt this time. His stomach was also a lot better. Ms. Brown, who said to call her Susan, took him to a cabin earlier that morning and fed him breakfast. She also gave him a change of clothes. The sweatpants were a little too big, but he pulled the drawstring tight and tied it in a knot. He got sleepy then and laid down on the couch. He didn't know how long he had slept, but it was still morning, and his stomach was still comfortably full from breakfast. He stirred as Susan reached down to lift him.

"We're going to see a lot of pretty country today," she said. Adam wasn't interested.

"If I'm really good and quiet today, can I please go home and see my parents?" Adam asked with a shaky voice. "I promise I'll be good. I just miss them…"

Sobs cut off his words. He cried harder than he had ever cried in his life. Harder than when he broke his arm while playing baseball and harder even than when his dog, Critter, got out and was hit by a car. Susan took him in her arms and tried to comfort him. Overwhelmed with grief, loneliness, and fear, he let her hold him as he drained himself of every last tear. Then he just sat quietly in her arms with his head on her shoulder. That's when he realized Susan was crying, too. That didn't help him at all. Everything is scarier when the grown-ups are crying.

"Nothing's going to happen to you, little guy," she whispered to him. "Jackson says you're very special. He has a test for you, and since you're very special, you'll pass that test. And when you pass the test, you'll get to go home. He promised me."

"Promise?"

"I promise."

Adam didn't know how good a promise from a kidnapper was, but it was all he had. He dried his face with his hand and walked outside with her.

The doctor from the sleep study was sitting in the driver's seat. Adam stopped walking and pulled at Susan's hand.

"What is he doing here?" Adam's voice was a whisper.

"That's Jackson. You remember him, don't you?" Susan replied. "Don't you worry about a thing. Did you know that you and Jackson are related?"

"No."

"Well, you are. And family takes care of family."

I want my real family. Adam was too afraid to say it out loud, so he kept quiet and climbed into the motorhome. He settled himself on the couch and put on the seatbelt. Under different circumstances, he would be interested in why motorhomes have seatbelts in the couches, but right now he had bigger things to think about.

"It took you guys a while," Adam heard Jackson say to Susan as she put on her own seatbelt.

"He had a little breakdown but it's better now," Susan said with a hushed voice. "There's no reason to have him worked up. It won't help a thing."

She was right about that. Being worked up wouldn't help anything. The only thing that would get Adam home is passing the test that they had for him. He didn't know what the test would be, but he had to pass it. He had to get home. He no longer worried that his parents wouldn't love him anymore because of his stupid mistake. They still loved him after he spilled an entire bucket of paint on the carpet. They even still loved him after he didn't close the door all the way and Critter got out. They would still love him after he got himself kidnapped.

At least, he hoped they would.

Susan closed her eyes and listened to the sound of the road under the tires. She was only vaguely aware of the voice in her mind. She could hear it clearly sometimes, but other times she forgot it was even there. Right now, she was tired and emotionally worn out. She didn't want to be bothered with thoughts, but it seemed it was when she was tired and worn out that the voice got through the loudest.

Grab the steering wheel, it told her.

Why? What good would that do?

You'd get off the road, it reasoned.

Susan looked at the road they were on. It curved up a hill and had only a small shoulder before a cliff on her side.

We'll go off the cliff.

That's better than going forward.

We'd die.

There was nothing, then a crystalline giggle like that of a child.

Susan closed her eyes and rubbed her forehead. Sometimes these conversations gave her a headache.

She wasn't sure when the conversations started, but they went as far back as she could remember. It was usually that voice in her head that got her into trouble. She'd be sitting quietly watching cartoons, her mind would wander, and soon she'd have thoughts of knocking over the television. *Do it and see what happens*, the voice would say. As she got older, the dares got worse. *Just try one puff and see if you like it.* Or while making out with her high school boyfriend, *bite his tongue and see what his blood tastes like.* Or in college, *who cares if he's married, give him what he wants so you can have what you want.* And later, *take the money, you earned it.* The times when Susan didn't do what the voice wanted, she would have thoughts of hurting herself.

Nobody wants you around. It would be easier if you just weren't here. Nobody likes you. Nobody wants you. Look at you. You're a hideous monster and you shouldn't be here. Just take those pills and it'll be better. Come to the Nothing. It wants you.

Since she met Jackson, her thoughts have been different. She thought less about hurting herself and focused on helping him with his research. *Find the right children. That one's not right. Find this boy, he's perfect. Find the boy. Find the boy.*

Take the boy.

And she did. She was surprised how much she wasn't upset about kidnapping a child.

She even smiled a little at the thought.

I'm his mother now. It's not kidnapping if he's with his mother.

She glanced over at Jackson.

But Jackson's not his father. Jackson is his brother.

And nobody knows it but me.

She gave a small, silent laugh at her private joke and looked out the window, a lock of amber hair twisting around her fingers.

Arlington, VA

Jack Cole looked across his desk at the agents in his office. He took his time thinking through his next few sentences. A doctor to stars and political high-powers for the last 40 years, he was a master at the art of thinking before every word. He also was quite skilled at winning people over. He would need both talents now.

"Thank you for coming to me privately with this. Your discretion is greatly appreciated." He paused and considered his next words before speaking. "It is true that in my younger days I had some indiscretions. I'm not aware of offspring from those times. It seems to me that if there was, someone would have come forward by now. But that aside, the accusations against my son are very serious, and most likely the result of malicious intent by a rival or some nonsense like that. I'm sure you will be conducting a thorough investigation *before* anything is said publicly."

"Yes, sir. An investigation is already underway. That's why we're here." The agent's tone was friendly but firm. "We can't locate your son and we hoped you may be able to tell us where he is."

Jack flipped through the pages of his desktop calendar.

"Yes. He's on his annual trip to Wyoming. I'm afraid I don't know more than that." Jack stood up to signal the end of the meeting. "I have another meeting starting soon and I wouldn't want them to overhear anything. I'm sure you can understand. Let's meet again in another three hours and we can exchange any information either of us may have."

They agreed and Jack shook their hands.

"And, gentlemen, my wife is a very kind and gentle person. She has loved me through my many faults, but she doesn't know about those 'indiscretions' we mentioned. It would hurt her very badly to find out now." Jack let the unspoken question linger.

"Of course. There's no need to mention anything about that at the moment."

Jack nodded in appreciation as he opened his office door for the men. As they left, he closed the door again and sat back down at his desk. He thought through the few half-truths in his responses and assured himself they would go unnoticed.

Jack did know about his two illegitimate children, though he knew little more than the fact that they existed. For him, they were only tied to salacious memories from trips out west.

The first, a son, was the product of an evening with a young office assistant. Jack was 34 at the time. She had just turned 21. Jack was visiting a friend from college who was working at a law firm in San Francisco. She was the friend's receptionist. He asked her for a good restaurant recommendation then invited her to come along since he didn't know the city. She was doe-eyed and happy to show her city to a newcomer. They shared expensive wine with dinner and an expensive hotel room after. She didn't make it to work the next day. He didn't know if it was a hangover or embarrassment over their one-night stand that kept her home. It didn't matter. It was his last day in town. His only disappointment was that he wouldn't get to bed her again.

Six months later, he came back for a conference. He was looking forward to another evening with the girl, but when she looked up from her desk and saw him, her expression was anything but welcoming. He noticed a wedding ring on her finger that wasn't there before. And when she stood up, he noticed much more. She was very far along in pregnancy, and he knew without a doubt it was his. She only said one sentence to him his entire visit.

"We never happened."

He later heard that she had quit her job and had a son. At the time, it hit Jack with a pang of guilt. Today, however, he couldn't even remember her name.

The second child was a daughter. Jack had known her mother well. He may have even loved her.

Rebecca was a free spirit, living just off the beach in a small house behind a storefront. Jack spent most of his life among the conservative circles of West Virginia and had never met anyone like her. In the 1980s world of punk music, loud cars, and brash people, Rebecca was an island of serenity. They met during the same visit when Jack learned the office assistant was pregnant. He had planned a weekend at the beach a few hundred miles down the coast from San Francisco. His fantasy had been to take the girl with him, but he was there alone. That was fine, too. He was never unhappy with his own company.

He sat at an outdoor café, watching the birds, and sipping coffee as a woman sat at the table next to him. She was about his age, mid-30s, with long sun-bleached hair that fluttered down her back with the pulse of the coastal breeze. Jack had been a young child during the days of the 1960's hippies, but with her long skirt and flowing top, that was the image that came to mind. She was a far cry from his world of business suits and power deals.

He watched as she dug in her large woven purse and pulled out an unusual deck of cards. She shuffled them several times, then shifted slightly in her chair to face Jack with a friendly and sincere smile.

"Would you like a reading?"

"I'm sorry, what?"

"A card reading."

"You're a fortune-teller?"

Jack didn't hide his surprise and distaste, but the woman met it with kindness.

"No. Fortune-telling is for fairs and movies. I use impressions and intuition to help you work through things that you aren't seeing clearly. Here," she moved to the chair across from him, "may I join you?"

"It seems you may," he said, noting that she had already sat down with him. Still, he was very intrigued by the woman. It was the gentleness of her spirit more than any physical quality that drew him in. "Please, go on."

"I can only read for you with your permission, so if you give me your permission, take the cards and shuffle them a few times. While you do, keep thinking about whatever it is that's troubling you."

Jack did as she instructed then handed the deck back to the woman. "How do you know something's troubling me?"

"That doesn't take a fortune teller to see. It's written in the wrinkles above your eyebrows."

Jack sensed she was teasing him. Instead of being offended, he felt more at ease. He suspected that was her intention. He watched as she laid several cards out in a cross shape on the table. Her smile was comforting.

"There is a heavy female influence in your reading." She playfully raised an eyebrow. "It appears those wrinkles in your forehead are caused by the ladies in your life. Your foundation is strong. You've always had a light shining on your path and you do not doubt which way to go. It's certainly not your career that troubles you."

Jack was amused by her reading, but she hadn't told him anything he didn't already know. She also had not asked for any money, so he let her continue.

"But still, there is a disruption about you. You're afraid of upsetting someone in your close circle. It almost frightens you." Rebecca looked nearly mesmerized as she looked from card to card. She tilted her head slightly and looked Jack in the eyes. "What could be frightening you?"

Jack didn't answer her question. Her gaze made him feel more vulnerable than he had in a long time, as if he sat there nude for all the world to see. Rebecca seemed comfortable in the silence and didn't press for an answer. He was grateful. After a long moment, she took a soft breath and gently placed her hand on top of his on the table. Her voice was nearly a whisper.

"See? No fortune-telling. Just some intuition about what's bothering you. Maybe it helped you see what you need to work through."

Jack felt close to tears as she gathered up her cards and placed them back in her purse. She smiled at him again.

"The first one's free. If you want to know more, I work across the street at the book shop." Rebecca held out her hand. "Thank you for spending some time with me."

He shook her hand, and she was quickly off to cross the street. He thought about her throughout the weekend but never went to find her at the bookstore. He wasn't one to let himself feel vulnerable around anyone. It took him another year to go back.

But when he did, the bookstore was the first place he went. She remembered him immediately.

"The lady's man is back. I didn't think you'd come through this way again." Her smile, as before, was warm and inviting. "I'm just closing up."

"Have dinner with me."

She paused for a moment then crossed the room to take his hands in hers.

"Make love to me first. Then there will be no pretending during dinner."

Jack was taken aback by her directness and yet was immediately aroused. "Here in the bookstore?"

"No. I rent the house out back."

"I don't even know your name."

"Has that stopped you before?" There was no judgment in her question, just an understanding that vaguely worried Jack. "I'm Rebecca. We can have dinner first if you like."

"I'm Jack. Why don't you show me your house?"

They didn't bother turning on the lights as they walked through the small, square house to the bedroom. They embraced each other with a hunger that led to a blur of clothes and flesh and long silky hair tangled around arms. Jack laid Rebecca on the bed as she pulled his body into hers. She was all passion and no regret. She knew exactly what she wanted, and it didn't scare her. She wasn't ashamed of her sexuality like the other women Jack had known.

The casual affair lasted for two years. Jack flew out to California every few months to visit. Rebecca always welcomed him into her home and into her bed, and she never asked too many questions. The last time they saw each other, she was pregnant. He had tried to accuse her of carrying another man's child, but he knew the truth. She knew it as well: He wouldn't be coming back to visit. They both said goodbye with tears in their eyes.

It was the only time Jack cried over a woman. He had slept with many. None came close to the experience he had with Rebecca. No one ever would.

It was more than 30 years ago, and even in his advanced age now, he felt his body responding to the memory of her. At his age, he thought that was pretty impressive. He indulged himself a few more seconds of the memory before turning his mind back to the matter at hand.

His orderly life had just become very messy, and once again it was Jackson's doing. His son would be the end of him one day. Jack already took medication for a heart condition.

He didn't need the stress of whatever situation Jackson was causing now.

San Francisco

"Talk to him."

"What do I say?"

"Tell him you love him and that we're coming to get him."

Thomas held a picture of Adam as he sat in the passenger seat of his car. Aurea was driving; He was too worn to concentrate on the road. He had not expected things to be easy when he explained the situation to his wife and the police. He was right. They went through the same realm of emotions and disbelief Thomas had. They only started to believe the story when he played the recorded call on his phone.

Thomas and Aurea talked privately with Thomas's wife. After quite a bit of convincing, the three agreed that Amanda would stay to work with the police and be a liaison between them and Thomas. Thomas and Aurea would head out in the direction of the last known location for Jackson Cole: Montana. No one would be speaking to the media. They all agreed it was the best plan for keeping Adam safe and getting him home.

Thomas hated leaving his wife to deal with this on her own. He hated not having her with him as he went. It was the worst moment of their lives and they needed each other. They were each other's fortress in hard times. He needed her as badly as she needed him. But Adam needed them both, and he needed them to do separate jobs now. So, that's what they would do. Amanda stayed at the house with both sets of grandparents there with her. Thomas packed a duffle bag while Amanda packed a bag for Adam.

"So that he'll have clean clothes and some books for the ride home," she said. Her face was red and swollen from hours of crying when she walked her husband to the door. Her expression was a mixture of worry, panic, and pained guilt. She blamed herself for giving the kidnappers access to her son. She sank into Thomas's arms as she pleaded one more time, "Bring our son back."

How often had he heard that in the emergency room? "Bring my child back!" Parents would plead with him, demand from him. Maybe in different words, but always meaning the same thing. Sometimes, he would hear their cries in his sleep.

Thomas and Aurea were now in his car, headed east. It would take them a full day and night of driving to get to Montana. They planned to do it in shifts, to make the best time possible. It was his turn to rest, but instead, he focused on the picture of his son. He longed to believe what Aurea was saying, that he could connect with his son from so far away, but he calloused against the idea.

"You've been talking to saints and angels your whole life. You believe they can hear you because they exist in the realm that's always all around us," Aurea told him as she drove.

"You mean Heaven?"

"Well, yes, but what I believe is that the realm isn't just for angels and saints. It's where we're all connected," she said.

"That sounds an awful lot like how you described what Jackson believes."

Aurea paused before speaking again.

"I suppose it is," she said. "It's all a lot alike, isn't it? I believe everything that ever existed is connected in the Akashic realm. Some call it 'Heaven'. Some call it the collective consciousness. It's all pretty much the same thing. It makes you wonder, doesn't it?"

"Wonder what?"

"We're all talking about the same thing, just using a different term for it. If we all realized that and stopped fighting over who was right, what would humankind accomplish?"

"You're oversimplifying it. You've completely left out theology." Thomas stared out the window for a moment before continuing. "People aren't just admitted into Heaven because they want to go. You must follow the Christian belief system."

"Yes, that's where we're different. We don't have to believe anything to be part of the Akashic realm. We're part of it because we exist, and we don't have to die to access it."

"I mean this in the gentlest way," Thomas said. "I'm going to stick to eternity in Heaven."

Aurea glanced over and gave him a friendly smile. He was pleased that he hadn't offended her. His faith wasn't shaken by their conversation, but as he rode in the car he wondered if it was at all possible to reach Adam with just his thoughts. Surely, God wouldn't mind if he tried.

Thomas closed his eyes and focused on a mental image of his son. With the voice of his thoughts, he spoke to him.

"I love you, Adam. Your mother and I love you very much. I'm coming to get you. You stay safe and Aurea and I will find you."

Not trusting his ability to reach this "connection" that Aurea talked about, Thomas repeated the message in his mind over and over until the mantra soothed him into sleep.

Aurea glanced sideways at Thomas as he drifted off. She was relieved to see his body relax into the seat as the physical need for rest took over. She felt her own body relax a little now that he was asleep. She planned to let him rest for as long as possible. Not only did Thomas need his strength, but Aurea needed some time to think.

As much as Thomas and his wife had been forced to learn and believe over the last few hours, things were also moving very quickly for Aurea. She suddenly had a child's life in her hands, a child she didn't even know. Still, yesterday she did see him in her meditative dream, then again in her nightmare. She knew he was in trouble and tried to comfort him.

She wasn't sure Thomas or his wife understood or believed anything she told them, but they were so desperate to find their son that they would do anything. She understood now why frauds could be successful in scams and lies that Aurea always thought seemed obvious. Desperate people were willing to grasp on to any hope.

But she wasn't a fraud and there were no lies or scams. This was all very real. Jackson had placed the mantle on her to save the innocent boy and return him to his innocent parents. Did Jackson know about her gift, or did he just really hate her and want to punish her along with Thomas? As Aurea thought it through, she decided that must be his motivation. Harming Adam would destroy Thomas. To also destroy Aurea, he had to make her responsible for Adam's death. The thought of her flaws or inabilities causing a child harm was torture.

Somehow from thousands of miles away, Jackson had managed to read everything so clearly. He had strong gifts, too. Aurea always assumed her gifts were from her mother. Now she wondered, how much had been passed down to her and her brothers from their paternal lineage.

She thought about it as she drove on Interstate 80 east from San Francisco. She was to drive the first shift and they'd change in Reno, Nevada. It was just over four hours, as long as the traffic held. It was midday on a Saturday, so there wasn't much commuter traffic to deal with. She was grateful for that, and for the five hours of sleep she got on the airplane the night before.

When she lived in California, she usually kept to the coast and never saw this stretch of the state. She was surprised by miles of land that held swaths of sunflowers, past their seasonal peak but still beautiful, and the tall grass of a wildlife reserve just before the first buildings of West Sacramento. The traffic picked up again as she headed into the city, but despite her last few years in a sparsely populated part of Minnesota, she was still a skilled city driver. She weaved effortlessly in and out of traffic and made good time through the area. Soon after, the traffic cleared, the interstate lost a couple of lanes, and the road started climbing up the pass through the Sierra Nevada. A road sign notified her she was on Donner Pass, named after the tragedy-destined group of travelers who tried to make it through the pass in the dead of winter with only their covered wagons. They became snowed in, and several resorted to cannibalism before dying themselves. Aurea shivered at the thought.

As she did, something caught her eye. A quick blur, like a deer about to run out into the road. Her reflexes were quick and smooth as she slowed the car. She checked the shoulder and didn't spot the animal. She glanced at Thomas to see if he was still asleep. She looked back at the road and there it was.

A child, not a deer.

A little girl with a pink nightgown and blonde hair stood directly in the car's path, just feet ahead.

Aurea slammed her foot hard on the brake pedal and pulled the steering wheel to the right. Tires squealed and the back of the car swung around out of her control.

A hollow thud.

Thomas was yelling.

The car skidded to a stop.

"What the hell was that?" Thomas yelled at her. A line of blood rolled down from his hairline.

Aurea's breathing was fast, her palms hurt from gripping the steering wheel, and she was completely paralyzed.

"Aurea! What the hell happened?" Thomas was still yelling. He grabbed her arm, hard. "What did you do?"

Aurea stuttered, "I-I don't know. There was a girl."

"Where? Did you hit her?"

"I don't know," Aurea whispered. She turned to Thomas but saw the car was empty. He was already out and headed to help the girl. She got out and found him behind the car.

"There's nobody there," he said. Aurea saw that he was right. The only thing on the road were the marks from their tires. Another car drove by and slowed down to look at them standing on the narrow shoulder. It continued without stopping.

"I heard it. Something hit," Aurea said, her voice weak.

"You heard me hitting my head." Thomas touched his wound and showed her the blood on his fingertips as if to prove that he was injured. "Did you fall asleep?"

"No," Aurea said, though her confidence wavered. "I don't think so."

Thomas walked to the driver's side of the car.

"It's not safe to stand here. Everything looks fine. Let's go," he said through clenched teeth. "I'm driving."

Aurea got in the passenger seat and put on her seatbelt. She looked at the small smear of Thomas's blood on the window and wanted to clean it off. She had some tissue in her purse, but she was afraid to move. Sitting next to Thomas when he was angry felt like sitting next to a deadly snake all coiled up and ready to strike.

She looked out the windshield and replayed the last few minutes in her mind. She had been wide awake; she was certain of that now. She saw a girl in the road. The girl stood there, staring at her, plain as day. Aurea felt another shiver run through her when she thought about the look on the girl's face.

She was smiling.

Chapter 7

Jack swirled the ice around in his glass and chilled the mahogany-colored liquid inside. It matched the deep, velvety brown shades of his home office quite well, and matched his extravagant tastes even better. The gentle, almost longing melody of one of Liszt's *6 Consolations* was the only sound in the room, save for the occasional clinking of ice on glass. He often listened to the piano solos when indulging in whiskey and deep thought. His wife never bothered him when she heard Liszt through the door.

He sat in the chair behind his desk and stared at one of the four filing cabinets across the room. They all matched his office furniture perfectly, made from fine wood in deep shades, standing tall and stately. He looked at the one on the right end. It was the only one with a lock, and it had been a long time since he unlocked it. Some things were better kept securely tucked away. Still . . .

Jack set his glass on a leather coaster on his desk, pulled open his top desk drawer, and retrieved a set of keys. He hesitated as he walked across the room, feeling almost fearful of what he would find even though he already knew what was there. He paused as he passed the door that led out into the rest of the house and clicked the lock on the handle, just in case his wife decided to come in despite hearing the music.

His feet felt leaden as he walked the final few steps to the filing cabinets. He maneuvered the key into the lock and turned it. The top drawer slid open ever so slightly, inviting him to dive into the records of all his sins.

They were all there. Thousands of pages of notes, all meticulously typed and preserved, the first drafts shredded or burnt out of existence. It was to be his big contribution to medicine, a study on how the minds of children, so pure and open to experience, could be exercised and shaped into grand machines of possibility.

It started with an admiration of child prodigies, like Mozart who started composing beautiful music at only five years old and Juana Ramírez de Asbaje who was born in the mid-1600s and amazed the world with her extraordinary intelligence. She is still remembered as one of the most important writers of Mexican literature of the Baroque period. Jack learned about the prodigies when he was a child, and desperately wanted to be named among them. He was always the brightest in his class and teachers lavished compliments on him, but he was never as intelligent as he wished. He had to be the best in all things, and it so very often seemed that there was someone, somewhere, who was better. It was exhausting.

In medical school, he learned the pleasure of helping other people. Sure, others would say the pleasure was in how good it felt simply to help someone live a healthy life. For Jack, it felt good when those people admired his skill and abilities. In the drawers of this now unlocked cabinet were the files that showed the extent to which he wanted to show those skills and abilities.

The one he wanted was in the drawer closest to the ground. He cursed the age of his knees and back as he bent slowly down to the drawer and opened it. He read the names on the tabs of the files and thumbed through the pages. He carefully pulled the file out of the cabinet and stood upright, his head a little dizzy from bending over.

When he sat back at his desk, he opened the file and found a picture of two young girls. Sisters. They sat side-by-side with smiles on their faces and hand-me-down coats over their shoulders. The younger one, a three-year-old, held a doll. The older girl, a five-year-old, had just lost her first tooth. Jack remembered how excited they were on that day when their mother brought them in to play in his office. That's all it was at first, just play. They played with toys and cards, with their mother sitting quietly in a chair in a corner of the room and Jack in a connecting room, observing through a window and listening through a speaker. A collection of lollypops sat in a mug on his desk, from which the girls could select a treat once they were done.

He got to know them very well over the next two years. They came in every week and performed his tasks so diligently. Their minds showed constant evidence of sharpening and every week he was excited about the results.

If he had left it at that, perhaps things would have ended differently. Their file would have ended like the dozens of others in that locked cabinet, with the children taking a final lollypop and the experiment ended.

But that wasn't the real test. He was certain he had found a way to not only make people smarter but to unlock that part of the brain that separates humans from Gods. That was what these sisters would help him prove. A year into his experiments with them, he started injecting the sisters with a mixture of chemicals that made the brain more active. It was mostly vitamins and amino acids that he tried, nothing that would get him into trouble. As he saw better results, he increased dosages and made changes to formulas. Only occasionally did it trouble him that he spent his days as a young internist, treating adults and their ailments, and his evenings as something of a mad scientist, creating concoctions and trying them on children.

He would of course lose his license and possibly go to jail if anyone ever found out, but he paid the mother handsomely and had her sign a non-disclosure agreement. The agreement wouldn't hold up in court, but she didn't know that.

He flipped through the pages of notes with all this incriminating evidence typed so clearly on them and wondered if now was the time to burn it all. Jackson had done something stupid and rash, and it sounded so familiar to Jack. Like the one night he had done something stupid and rash and a young girl died.

The girl in the file, in the photograph that he held again in his hand, had died on a bed in his medical office. He had miscalculated his formula. That's what he told himself over and over when guilt rose up. In truth, he had misjudged his own intelligence and his experiment was a failure. He altered medical records to show that the girl died from unmanaged diabetes, so there was no follow-up and no questioning.

Everything stopped then. Jack was devastated, not so much at the loss of the child, but because he had proven himself to be wrong. Possibly even foolish, if he thought such a thing was possible. He cleaned up his notes and filed them away in a locked cabinet.

The mother was beyond herself with grief, which she tried for years to drown in bottles of cheap gin, and never questioned the doctor's diagnosis. He didn't know what happened to the younger sister. He assumed she probably ran away and became a drunk like her mother.

With that thought, he poured himself another whiskey and contemplated how he could burn the files without his wife seeing.

Western North Dakota

Jackson looked out over the horizon. It was easy to see why the place had earned the title of the Badlands. It stretched as far as the eye could see, these rocky hills with sharp cliffs, grass-covered plateaus, and valleys dotted with sagebrush and wildflowers. It was devastatingly beautiful, but for anyone trying to cross on foot or horseback, it would have been a difficult and dangerous ride. It was the perfect place for Jackson to begin his experiment.

"Adam, look around. What do you think of this place?"

"I don't know," Adam said as he took in the area, moving only his eyes. Jackson noticed the boy's pale face and stiff posture.

"It's okay. You only have to look at it." Jackson tried to be comforting, but it wasn't something that came naturally to him. He would have to try harder. This wouldn't work if Adam was too afraid to concentrate right now. Fear would come later; For now, Adam needed to be calm.

They were parked at a scenic overlook within the Theodore Roosevelt National Park. The tourist season had ended just a few weeks before, and now the park was nearly deserted. On the off chance they did pass another car on the winding road through the park, the motorhome kept them disguised as just another family out for a trip together. The motorhome took up a good portion of the available parking space at this overlook, so Jackson suspected even if there were other visitors, no one else would be stopping. He set up a couple of chairs outside the motorhome as Susan cooked something on the stove for dinner.

"The sun will be setting soon. It'll look stunning from here," Jackson said. He motioned for Adam to sit in the chair next to him. "What do you know about science?"

"I don't know," Adam said. "I watch the science guy on T.V."

"Good. That's good," Jackson knew it was important to make a connection with people to bring them around to his way of thinking. "I bet the science guy likes to do experiments. All good scientists do. We're going to do an experiment."

"Is that the test?" Adam asked.

"It is. I knew you were a very smart boy. Your part of the experiment is going to be very easy. All you have to do is look at this land," he motioned to the horizon, "concentrate on it and tell Aurea about it. You remember Aurea from your dreams?"

"Yes, but how am I going to tell her about it? I don't know where she is. I don't have her phone number."

"That's the science. You're going to tell her with your mind." Adam's expression turned incredulous as Jackson continued. "The human mind is capable of so much more than what we use it for. Throughout all of history, we've seen instances that show this. Now it's our turn to prove it. That's why I brought you here first. There aren't very many places around that look like this. You're going to practice tonight with sending this thought to Aurea."

"What happens after that?"

"Then we go to the real experiment."

"What if I can't do it?"

The question irritated Jackson, but he fought to keep it out of his voice.

"Adam, there are times in our lives when failing isn't an option. I have staked everything on you being able to do this. You won't let me down." Jackson relaxed into his chair. It was true; Adam wouldn't let him down. Either the experiment would work, and Jackson's genius would be proven, or Adam's death would torture those Jackson wanted to hurt. Either way, Jackson would be happy.

And he's not the only one.

"If you'll excuse me, Adam, I need to take a walk. If Susan asks where I am, tell her I had to find a cell signal and make a call. I won't be too long."

Jackson watched the bars on the cell phone until he found a strong enough signal for a call. He had Susan buy the phone before she picked up the boy so they would have something untraceable to use. He dialed and waited for the voice on the other end.

"I'm glad you called. How's it going?"

"Things are going well here. Have you heard anything?"

"Yes, they're looking for you, but they think you're in Montana. Don't sit still too long."

"We won't. The boy will do well."

"Good. Call me tomorrow. You know how I worry."

"I will."

"Document everything. An experiment is only as good as the notes."

"I know."

"And, Jackson, tie up that loose end."

Jackson shut off the phone and removed the battery just in case someone tried to ping its location. They would need to get back on the road soon. It wouldn't do to have the experiment interrupted.

Idaho Falls, Idaho

Thomas put his cell phone on speaker and counted how many times it rang. It was answered on three.

"Hello, son. Any news?" Gabriel's voice was eager, but still soothing to Thomas's ear.

"No. How about there?"

"Nothing so far."

"How's Amanda? I tried her cell first, but it went straight to voicemail." Thomas was worried about his wife and the baby she carried.

"She's fine. We made her turn off her phone and lay down for a while. She needed some rest."

Thomas's shoulders relaxed just a bit and his voice softened. "Thank you for being there."

"Where else would I be?" Gabriel asked. "How about you? Where are you guys now?"

"We've stopped to rest somewhere in Idaho, at a roadside motel." Thomas looked around the small room. It was dark and decorated in the oranges and browns of the 1970s. Rather than being retro, he was sure it just had never been updated. It was clean and inexpensive, and that's all that mattered right now. "I wanted to keep going, but we're both exhausted. I think Aurea may have fallen asleep a little while driving. She nearly drove us off the road."

"What's she like? Do you think she's part of this? We've all been wondering about it here. Are you safe with her?"

Thomas sat on the bed. He took the phone off speaker and lowered his voice, just in case Aurea could hear from the room next door. The walls seemed pretty thin.

"No, I don't think she's part of it, but she's definitely a little strange. One of those free-love pagan types that you see on Hippie Hill." It was a place he visited once or twice in college, where San Francisco's hippie movement was still thriving.

"Oh, man, that place is trouble," Gabriel said. "But don't ever tell your mother that I know that."

Thomas smiled at Gabriel's effort to comfort him. "I won't."

"Speaking of staying out of trouble, Father David came by a little bit ago. We told him in confidence that you had a lead on who may have Adam. There are many prayers being said for Adam, and for you."

Thomas knew that should be reassuring, but he was numb to feeling it. Gabriel must have sensed it through Thomas's silence.

"Thomas, you're in a very dark time. We all are. We're all very vulnerable right now," Gabriel said. "When we're vulnerable like this, it's the easiest time for the Devil to come in and get us to start doubting God's love for us. Don't let that happen."

Thomas let a brief moment pass before speaking. "I won't."

Western North Dakota

Adam kicked a pebble on the roadway. He thought about running for help, but they were in the middle of nowhere. He could see for miles and there wasn't a single building around. There were hills and canyons and a lot of rocks, but nothing of any use. If he wandered off, he would die out there.

A few minutes ago, he heard a car coming. He thought about flagging it down and screaming for help, but before he could decide if he was brave enough to do it, the sound of the car faded off. It must have taken a different road. The small outlook they were at didn't get much traffic.

There wasn't a soul around to help him.

Susan hummed something as she cooked inside on the small stove in the motorhome. Adam smelled the sweet scent of onions and butter coming out of the tiny window where she stood. He hated onions. Still, his stomach growled with the anticipation of food. He glared up at the window with a hatred for the woman.

Immediately after, he felt guilty for it.

I bet she knew he was going to take me and she came along to make sure I'm okay, he decided. He decided Ms. Brown, *Susan*, was on his side because she couldn't be a bad guy.

He was suddenly grateful to have her there with him. He wouldn't even complain about the onions.

That decided, Adam looked around him once again. He'd better start figuring out how to have special powers. He held his arms out in front of him and made a frame with his hands, the way he'd seen artists do on old TV shows. That's what he would do. He would make a painting in his mind and focus on that.

He started with the sky. The sun was just getting to the horizon behind him, and it cast bright orange and yellow light over the hills in front of him. The hills weren't gigantic like the mountains in California. But they were too big to climb, at least for a kid. He was sure a grown-up could climb one of the hills in an afternoon. That's if they were rock climbers like the people on TV, and not prone to stepping wrong and spraining their ankle like his mom did.

The tears were instant.

No, don't think about it. Don't think about home. Just focus.

There was a weird black line that curved around the bottom of all the hills. They were just learning about geology at school and had learned that mountains had layers of different types of rocks and things. Now that he was paying attention, he could see several lines of layers around the hills.

There was the black line and some lines of brown, then some rows of gray, followed by what looked like light brown or even white. Toward the top, the layers became pink and red. His teacher would really like these hills.

He saw movement a long distance away to the left and watched the cluster of black dots move around. He soon realized there were several clusters, some far, and as he turned, some much closer. As he watched, he heard the hard snort of a large animal come from the right. He turned his head.

A giant, dirty beast stared at him from across the road.

It was dark and wide and taller than Adam's dad – or any person he could think of for that matter. The whole body was too much to take in, so Adam concentrated on the beast's giant head, which was covered in curly black fur. It had eyes bigger than Adam's fists and a snout the size of Adam's face. That alone was terrifying, but it was worse when Adam spotted the beast's horns. They stuck out of its gigantic head, big and thick and curved.

Adam suddenly had the urgent need to pee. The beast stomped its foot and Adam's bladder nearly released. He stopped the flow just in time.

Go away. Just turn and go away.

He wasn't sure if he was talking to himself or urging the beast to move. Either way, he knew the standoff needed to end. He took a small, slow step backward.

The beast flinched at the movement.

Go grab its tail.

The thought surprised Adam. It shot through his mind like someone had whispered it in his ear. Worse, the thought was tempting, and he had the urge to follow through. He stood there, unsure for just a second which way his feet would take him.

It was the beast that moved first.

With a loud, ugly grunt, it dipped its head and stepped forward. It was now only a couple of car lengths away from the boy, with nothing in between to stop it. The muscles in the side of the beast's body flexed and rippled like it was tensing and preparing to charge. Adam's breath stopped and his vision blurred. His chest hurt with the beating of his heart and his fingertips throbbed with the urgent pulse of his blood. He closed his eyes so he wouldn't have to watch the beast's attack.

Just go away. GO AWAY! He thought it over and over for as long as he could.

Adam's head was dizzy, and he finally let out his breath as he opened first one eye, then the other, to see why the beast wasn't charging.

It was gone.

Adam stared at the empty space in the road where the beast had been, then looked around for where it went. He saw no sign of the monster.

In the time that he had stood there staring down the beast, the sun had set and the light was going dim. It would be very dark soon, and Adam suddenly wished he had watched the beast walk off.

It was worse not knowing what was in the dark with you.

Susan turned an overhead light on and smoothed the wrinkles out of the map she placed on the motorhome table. She had a rough approximation of where they were in the North Unit of Theodore Roosevelt National Park. She would have preferred to use the GPS on her cellphone, but she didn't have a signal.

"If my math is right, it should take us a little over three hours to get to the South Unit tomorrow," she said to Jackson. "It looks like a pretty easy drive. About two hours to get out of this unit, then just over an hour south to the next unit."

"You're math is right. I already calculated the drive when I chose the locations." Jackson sounded disinterested in her observations.

"Of course you did. I just wanted to double-check, because sometimes things are different once you're actually on the road," Susan explained.

Jackson looked up at her from his seat across the table and gave her the small smile she was so fond of. "You're right. It's good to check things over now that we're actively in the experiment. Thank you for doing that."

His eyes were locked on hers and Susan felt a flutter in her chest. If they didn't have a small child playing outside, she might have thrown herself across the table. She felt a blush rise to her cheeks and turned her head to look out the window, hiding her desire by checking on Adam.

"It's getting dark. He should come inside now," she said as she stood up and walked to the door. She opened it and found Adam rushing toward her. "Hey buddy, what's chasing you?"

"What?" Adam sounded terrified as he whipped around to look behind him.

"No, it's just a saying. There's nothing there." Susan realized she had scared the boy and felt terrible about it. She bent down and hugged him as he stepped inside. "I'm so sorry about that. There's nothing out there. You were just coming up so fast."

"I thought I saw something," Adam said.

"Shh, it's okay. There's nothing there." Susan pulled back and smoothed Adam's hair out of his eyes. "The sun's going down. That's when the animals get more active. You probably saw a deer or something. Or maybe a wild horse. Wouldn't that be lucky? I've always wanted to see a wild horse. I've heard they have them here."

She didn't know why she was babbling, but it seemed the more words she said, the more Adam relaxed. She guided him over to the table and folded up the map. "I made us some spaghetti. You like spaghetti, don't you?"

Adam nodded.

"I thought so. Most kids like spaghetti. It took forever to boil the water on this stove, but I think everything turned out okay." She was talking too much again. She knew Jackson didn't like too much talking, but it seemed to comfort Adam. She dished up plates for the three of them and set them on the table. Before she took her seat, she started music playing on her cell phone and set it on the counter. Jackson had a problem with the sounds of people eating, so Susan played music at mealtimes to make him more comfortable.

"I don't have a cell signal, so we're stuck with the music I have saved on my phone. That means tonight's entertainment is classic boy bands of the early 2000s." Susan smiled at Adam and sat down beside him at the table.

It was only a short time later that dinner was cleared and put away, and they took turns changing in the bathroom to get ready for bed. Susan wore flannel pajamas. She gave Adam a fresh t-shirt and sweatpants to wear. She didn't know what

Jackson wore to bed; he closed the door to his little room in the back of the motorhome and she knew she wouldn't see him again until morning. She put a sheet and blanket on the couch for Adam, then converted the table area to her bed. Jackson wanted her in the main room with Adam to make sure he didn't run off in the middle of the night. Susan preferred it this way, too. It would be inappropriate for her to sleep in the same bed as Jackson with a child in the next room. It would also be extremely awkward for their first time in a bed together. That wasn't what she envisioned for a romantic evening. So, instead, she was fighting with a sheet as she tried to make her bed.

"Susan?" Adam's voice was quiet from the couch behind her.

"Yes?"

"Do you know Sarah?"

Susan froze in her spot, bent over the converted table-bed, sheet in hand. "Is she a girl from school?"

"No. She talks to me when I'm sleeping."

Even Susan's breath stopped for a moment. "What does she say to you?"

"She wants me to come play with her. She's all by herself."

Susan turned around and sat on the bed, facing Adam. He was laying on his back, facing up at the ceiling as he spoke. They both talked in whispers to avoid Jackson hearing. Susan struggled for something to say, but it was Adam who spoke again.

"She says she's bringing me to her, that you're taking me to her. Is that where we're going?"

"No, it's not," Susan reassured him. "Adam, are these the dreams you've been having that have frightened you? The dreams your parents were worried about when we first met?"

Adam's voice softened even more. "Yes."

Susan was hesitant, but had to ask, "Adam, what does Sarah look like?"

She listened as Adam described the same blonde-haired little girl she had seen standing next to his bed all those evenings ago. Somewhere inside of her, she had known for years that it was the same little girl who used to sit behind her, watching T.V. and combing her hair. The same little girl who even now still whispered thoughts of trouble in her ear.

Was that why the whispers wanted Adam?

It couldn't be. She had found Adam on her own. Jackson wanted a special child for his experiment, and she knew where to look.

But, how did she know?

"Adam, I'm going to always protect you." Susan kneeled on the floor next to Adam's bed and brushed his hair off his face. "You don't have to worry about anything as long as I'm here, alright?"

"Okay."

Susan took that as a cue that the conversation was over, as Adam rolled over on his side. She sat back on her own bed and tried to make sense of her thoughts.

This whole experiment was to prove that people can connect with each other using only their minds. Jackson would call it their consciousness, which he says survives even after a person's body is dead. If that is true, then couldn't a dead person send thoughts to a living person? The living person's mind would have to be open to it, and our minds are most open when we're asleep. When we're awake, the mind is very busy. Except when we're meditating. The mind is open during meditation. And prayer. In terms of the mind, prayer is a focused meditation. During these times, are we open to hearing whatever the dead want to tell us?

She thought about it as she settled into the small bed. It could create a new spin on Jackson's experiment, but she knew he wouldn't like it. It was too mystical. Perhaps she could find a way to look into this on her own. She would have to give it more thought, and for now, she had other things to worry about.

Sarah.

Is she real? And if she is, is she a threat to Adam? Jackson assured her no harm would ever come to the boy, and that she was there to make sure of it. She thought about it for another minute, then realized where her thoughts were leading her.

This is ridiculous. I'm worried about a ghost. There's no such thing as ghosts.

Even as she tried to comfort herself, she didn't fully believe it. It took her a long time to fall asleep, and when she did, her dreams were empty.

Chapter 8

Thomas typed a name into the search bar on his phone's internet browser. *Dr. Jack Cole.* If he was really the illegitimate offspring of the doctor, he wanted to know more about him. There were numerous news and magazine articles that mentioned the doctor, but it was an old video clip Thomas selected. In it, the doctor was featured in a news segment on nutrition. He was relaxed and comfortable in front of the camera. Thomas was surprised that he never noticed how much he resembled the man. Their hair color was starkly different, with Thomas's an ashy blonde and Dr. Cole's a deep black. Still, their stature, jawline, and other features were strikingly similar. In the time since this video clip, the doctor's hair had turned pure white, which Thomas thought made them look even more alike.

Thomas only watched the video for a few seconds. It felt like a morbid curiosity to see what this man was like. He went back to the search results and scrolled through as he looked for any information that may help him find his son. On the second page of results, he found the website for the doctor's practice. He clicked the link and looked through the site. It was as glossy and polished as the doctor himself. Thomas clicked the "contact" button and found a page with a phone number to the doctor's office.

It was morning as he sat on the edge of the bed in the roadside motel in Idaho Falls and stared at the phone in his hands. Should he call the office? Would he even be there? If he was there, would he even help Thomas? Why would Jake Cole go against the child he raised to help the child he abandoned?

What would it hurt to try?

Thomas called the number. Before the final note of the first ring, he ended the call. This man couldn't help him.

He swore as he threw the phone hard onto the bed. His anger swelled and he paced around the small room, aching for a way to physically express it. He wanted to punch and break things, to destroy everything around him. He grabbed the lamp off the nightstand and felt its weight in his hands as he went into his breathing routine. He was poised to shatter it against the wall, but instead, he held it firm as he breathed in for a slow count of four and out for another slow four-count. He told himself it wouldn't help anything to get arrested for busting up a motel room, and eventually set the lamp back on the nightstand.

He needed to get out of this space. It was time to get back on the road, even if they weren't sure where they were heading.

Theodore Roosevelt National Park, North Unit, Western North Dakota

Jackson watched Susan help Adam fold his bedding as they got ready to leave. It concerned him how attached she was becoming to the boy. She had never shown any motherly instincts with the other children they had seen in their offices, and she was downright irritable when he told her his plan to have her work at a school. It surprised him that she had taken to the boy so quickly. It was good to keep the boy calm, but if it continued it could affect the study results.

Worse, he was concerned about the conversation he overheard the night before. The boy was having bad dreams, and from the sound of Susan's voice last night, it rattled her. She vowed to protect the boy, and it sounded like she meant it. Jackson worried she forgot the goal of the experiment, which was to put the boy in peril and see how strongly he reacted. She couldn't be there protecting the child.

He thought about it as he drove to the South Unit of the national park. The whole trip took about three hours, and by the time they finally parked at an overlook for lunch, even Jackson was ready to be outside for a while.

"You can play outside, but stay close," he told Adam as the boy gathered some of the toy cars from his backpack. The last thing Jackson needed was for the child to get lost at the wrong time. "Susan and I have some work to go over."

Jackson saw Susan glance at him as she set up her laptop computer on the table. He retrieved his from the bedroom area where he kept his things and joined her.

"How do you think he's doing?" Jackson asked. He watched her body language as much as he listed to her answer.

Her gaze went out the window to where the boy played. She took a deep breath and placed her right hand on her left shoulder as if rubbing a kink out of the muscle. It was a basic subconscious self-soothing gesture that many people do without realizing when they're feeling tense. Jackson made a mental note of it.

"He's stressed but adjusting. I'd say he's doing well under the circumstances," she said.

Jackson decided to pry further. To lessen the impression of interrogation, he typed some things on his computer and kept his eyes on the screen as he spoke.

"I heard you two talking last night, just the sounds of voices, of course," he said nonchalantly. "Was it anything important?"

"No, not really."

Susan stopped rubbing her shoulder and started typing on her own computer. Jackson recognized the abruptness of it as a change in what Susan was feeling. She had been in need of comfort. Now, she wanted the focus off of the conversation. What was it she didn't want to talk about? Jackson stopped his own typing and looked directly at her. It was his physical cue for her to continue. It only took a moment for her to feel the weight of his stare.

"His nightmares are continuing, but that's to be expected," she said with a shrug of her shoulders. "He's in a high-stress situation. He's a child. He's going to have bad dreams. That's all it was."

Jackson thought for a moment. "Make sure to make a note of that in your written observations."

That was the end of the conversation. Jackson knew more from her body language than her words that Susan was worried about the boy. Worry is an emotion. Scientists were not to have emotions about their subjects. It always tainted the results. He would have to do something about that very soon.

Idaho

The cool air felt good on Aurea's skin. They were back in the car, and she had her window down for some fresh air. Thomas was driving again. He didn't trust Aurea at the wheel since her trouble back on Donner Pass. Aurea rolled her eyes at the thought. He would have done the same thing if he thought he saw a kid in the road.

They passed a road sign that indicated they'd soon be crossing into Montana. It didn't feel right to Aurea, but she had nothing to go on. So, they continued. The road felt unending at the moment. A continuous line of black asphalt, white and yellow lines, cars and trucks all on their own missions, and Aurea and Thomas attempting the impossible. The familiar drab of hopelessness crept into Aurea. She was too familiar with this feeling, no, this *anti-feeling,* of hopelessness, that filled the body with the weight of emptiness and stole all emotions. That's why it's an *anti-feeling*, she decided, because it makes you unable to feel. There's the hint of deep sadness that always bubbles up, but even that takes too much effort to feel against hopelessness.

And so, it all cancels each other out and leaves no feeling at all.

And here Aurea was, drowning in it once again.

She felt it for many months after the death of her mother. It came on after the first weeks of the initial shock and shattering grief that left her unable to do much of anything. That dulled down as she had to get back to some type of life, but it never left. Eventually, it turned into the *anti-feeling*. That, too, faded after many months, but every now and then it swept over her again, just as fresh. It smothered her today.

"What's on your mind?" Thomas interrupted her thoughts. His voice was more gentle than she'd heard from him before.

"Nothing much."

"You look so sad. Are you okay?"

Aurea turned slightly away from him and thought for a moment before answering. She stared at the radio speaker on the door to help keep her emotions in check.

"I was thinking about my mom, about grief. It never goes away, the grief," she said. "It's like a hum on the radio. It's loud and it's the only thing you can hear at first. Then, after a while, it dies down and you can hear the music over it. Eventually, it's still there, but you don't notice it unless you think about it. But sometimes, that hum just pops up loud again and you have to get back to the point where you know it's there, but it's in the background and you can hear the music again."

Aurea looked back out the window at the road. "That probably doesn't make any sense."

"Yes, it does. It makes perfect sense."

They rode in silence for the next many miles, both of them lost in their thoughts. As it turned to evening, they were finally in Montana. They found another motel to stop at so they could get some proper rest, even if just for a few hours. They also needed some food, showers, and to make phone calls. Thomas needed to call his wife and she had calls of her own to make, such as to the neighbor who was caring for her animals.

Once she was settled in her room, Aurea unpacked a few items from her bag. She took out a small incense holder and a cone of sandalwood incense. She set it safely on top of the dresser and lit it. A small stream of scented smoke drifted up and spread the light scent. She'd have to air out the room later, but she didn't mind. The scent helped her focus her mind. She sat on the edge of the bed and cleared her mind. She inhaled deeply, letting the familiar scent of sandalwood fill her. She relaxed her shoulders as she let thoughts enter and leave her mind. She sat for many minutes until the hopelessness she'd felt all day finally faded. By the time it had, the incense had burned itself out. She lit another and retrieved a deck of cards from her bag.

Different from the traditional Tarot cards the old woman at the conference had read several days ago, Aurea used a deck created around the Akashic realm. Instead of things like The Devil and The Tower, it had cards representing different messengers like archangels. Aurea relied primarily on her intuition, but the cards helped her focus that intuition at times when meditation on its own wasn't working.

She lit another incense cone for good measure and sat down at the small table in her room. It felt good to have the cards in her hands. As she shuffled them, she thought about

Adam and Jackson and where they may be. She thought about Thomas and his wife, and how they must be feeling. Then, she thought about herself and how she could possibly be of any help. After several minutes of shuffling, she laid a single card in front of her.

It showed a woman standing on a path in a forest. Before her, the path split into two. From where she was standing, the woman could not see that the path on the left was clear and bright, while the path on the right led to darkness and destruction. The card symbolized having to make a choice and the importance of choosing wisely.

Aurea looked at the card with frustration. It told her the one thing she already knew. She had to figure out which way to go. She put the cards away and laid down on the bed to clear her mind once more.

Western North Dakota

Adam stayed close by the trailer all evening. After lunch, they drove several miles to a different part of the national park. Adam watched out the window as they drove and saw several giant creatures like the one that had scared him the day before. He wasn't going anywhere near them.

He wished he could take a bath before bed. He didn't normally care to, but he'd been in this motorhome for several days now and after playing outside the last two days, he was pretty dirty. Susan always had him wash his hands before eating, but there wasn't much water for baths or showers. At least there was a bathroom, and he could have privacy when he used it. There was even a lock on the door.

He thought about these things as he lay in bed that evening. Susan and Dr. Cole were still doing some work at the table, but Adam was tired so he went to bed. Plus, the sooner he went to bed, the sooner the next day would come. And then he'd be one day closer to going home. The thought of home again instantly stung his eyes with tears. He rolled over and faced the wall so Dr. Cole wouldn't see him crying. He couldn't stop the tears this time, but at least he was able to keep them hidden. He clenched his eyes shut and let the tears fall silently onto his pillow.

Susan watched Adam fall asleep. He had eaten his dinner enthusiastically, and she was pleased to see his appetite return. He hadn't been hungry for lunch earlier. It was already late when they ate the hamburgers she had fried on the stove. She remembered Jackson ordering grilled onions on a hamburger during one of their rare meals together, so she made sure she had onions to grill for him.

It surprised her, how much she liked the feeling of being domestic. Maybe, if her life had been different, she could have had her own family complete with a husband and a son to care for. But that was not the life she had. She never dwelled on it before this. Except once, when she was pregnant with the child of a married man. A man with bright blue eyes, like Jackson's. Like Adam's.

She wished Adam would wake up and want her to hold him as he did earlier. She needed to be needed by him. Instead, it was Jackson who needed her now. He touched her on the shoulder and motioned silently for her to come outside with him. She followed, as she always did when he called.

The night was cold and dark out here in the middle of nowhere. They were still parked at the overlook, which Susan thought was probably prohibited, but there were no signs that said they couldn't overnight there. She wished she'd grabbed her coat before she went outside, but she didn't want to go back in for it now. Jackson so rarely needed her attention, she was afraid to break whatever spell he was under. She walked next to him as he led her down the road, away from the camper. She glanced over her shoulder, worried that Adam would wake up and be afraid.

"It's okay. We won't be long," Jackson assured her. "I didn't want to wake him up, so I thought we'd come over here and talk."

Susan's heart leaped, the way a schoolgirl's does when a crush notices her. It wasn't like Jackson to be romantic, and this was the most romantic setting she could imagine. The stars danced above them, a gentle breeze rustled through the sagebrush on the side of the road, and there was no one around to interrupt them.

Jackson took her to the side of the road and looked out over the landscape. She followed his eyes and saw that even in the darkness it was beautiful. She shivered as he touched her shoulder again and gently turned her to face him. He cupped his hand around the back of her neck and she lifted her face, ready for his lips on hers as his thumb stroked the delicate skin of her throat. Her body was suddenly warm in the cold night and a bead of sweat left an electric line down her back as she waited and anticipated his kiss.

The movement of his body matched her own deep, heavy breaths, and she saw a rare expression of excitement as Jackson tightened his hold on her neck and leaned into her. She reached up and put her hands on his arms, for the first time noticing the firmness of his biceps. She tapped his arm as his grip firmed even more.

It's too much.

She tapped his arms again, to cue him that his grip was too strong.

Why won't he stop?

"You're hurting me." That's what she meant to say, but it came out in gurgles and gasps.

Susan slapped aimlessly at Jackson and clawed at his hands—both hands, now—that were wrapped around her throat. She didn't understand what was happening, she only knew she had to get away from it, from him. She kicked her feet and only then realized she was somewhat off the ground. Her vision went red; she didn't know why. She told her body to breathe, but no air could get through the vice around her neck. Where was Jackson? Why wouldn't he help her, she wondered. Her panicked mind forgot it was he who was hurting her.

Until she remembered the boy in the camper. She was the only protection he had.

Oh God! Adam...

Many thoughts flashed through her mind and then she remembered another child that she didn't save: her sister, Sarah.

Sarah told her stories before bed, scary stories of falling asleep and never coming back. Sarah said it would happen. Sarah was there.

Susan thought again of Adam.

Then, there was nothing.

Except for the scent of peppermint.

Life is a strange thing, so fragile but fierce. It is a light easily snuffed out but protected at great measures. Jackson contemplated these things as he held Susan's life in the balance.

After the boy fell asleep, he lured her away from the motorhome with the promise of romance under the night sky. And wasn't death romantic? It brings such closeness to two otherwise unconnected beings. Just now, Jackson stared into Susan's eyes, wide with surprise and fear, and watched the flurry of emotions that ran through them. At first, trust and tenderness, but as his grasp around her neck turned from gentle to merciless, her face showed flashes of fear. Finally, in her last grasps at life, she showed understanding and betrayal. She must have realized that this was always part of the plan, and all the things Jackson promised her were lies.

He felt no remorse. It wasn't that her life had no value, but rather that he had no emotional attachment to it. Jackson felt that way about all life. When we lived, we lived. When we died, we died. Death was needed in the natural order of things. He learned early on not to form an emotional attachment to other people; it always led to pain or disappointment. He had no appetite for it, or for any of its physical manifestations for that matter. Still, he would use life, love, and even sex, to expand his understanding of the universe.

Now, he watched Susan's body stop living and wondered if he could communicate with her mind even though her body was dead. *Why bother, when she's finally quiet?* His dilemma now was what to do with the body. It needed to be hidden until the right time. It would make a nice calling card to let Aurea know she was on the right track. Even if it was discovered before she got there, the news of the body found at the National Park would be enough. Earlier, he spotted a small ledge just over the side of the overlook. He could walk down easily enough by himself, but bodies were much more difficult to move than they appeared to be in movies. He wouldn't want to misstep and hurt himself. He dragged Susan's body to the approximate spot and rolled her over the side. Maybe it would look like she jumped or just fell while looking over the edge. Maybe the animals would get to her before anyone found her. Whatever happened, it didn't matter. He would be miles away, preparing Adam for what comes next.

Butte, Montana

Aurea awakened with a sense of urgency.

"It's not Montana."

She turned on the bedside lamp and found the notepad and pen she had placed on the table earlier.

Earlier, after the disappointing card reading, she had laid on the bed to relax her thoughts again. After a few short minutes, exhaustion took over and she fell asleep.

That's when the communication came in waves of images.

A horizon of light-colored hills that almost look blue and pink, the soft, dusty colors of rock and dirt. That horizon was so vast, that it looked like nothing could possibly be beyond it. A cluster of trees showcased the vibrant colors of fall. Closer, the soft green of sagebrush and white wildflowers dotted the landscape. Over to the left, little prairie dogs popped their heads in and out of mounds of dirt. Some stood on hind legs and made sounds to communicate with each other. The image brought a quick sensation of enjoyment, but it didn't last long. To the right, some distance off, a monster of an animal stood like a giant on the road. Dark, matted fur covered its giant body. Large horns curved out of its head and ended in deadly points. The monster brought with it the feeling of fear and death.

Aurea knew instantly it was the North Dakota badlands she saw in her dream. She visited the area a couple of times a year. She also had seen many bison there, some very close up from the safety of her car. She knew what those monsters were. But Adam didn't. And that's how she was sure the vision came from him.

She wrote it down, put on clean clothes, and called Thomas on his cell phone. She glanced at the clock as the phone rang. It was four in the morning, but she knew he would not mind her waking him.

"I know where they are. Or, at least, where they were."

"I can be ready in five minutes. I'll meet you at the car."

Thomas was already waiting when she got to the parking lot. She threw her bags in the trunk with his and got into the passenger seat.

"They're in North Dakota."

"Are you sure? How do you know?"

"It was very clear. I was seeing the Badlands, a place I go to every spring and fall. They're unmistakable. It makes sense when you think about it. Jackson took Adam to a place I know, someplace unmistakable. It's the first step in a process: Make the first task something that can be solved fairly easily."

"The first task?"

Aurea rubbed her temples, an unfruitful attempt to quell the dull pain that throbbed there.

"I'm afraid so. This was almost too easy. It feels like we're being set up for something more difficult. A bigger challenge. Jackson is out to prove something big, life-changing. I doubt he will make it this simple for us and call it quits. We haven't proven anything, yet."

They both sat quietly with their thoughts as they drove. It would take about nine hours to get across the border into the North Dakota badlands. Would Adam still be there?

She feared she already knew the answer.

They watched the morning sun cross the sky into afternoon as they drove. They stopped only when necessary and pushed the limits of the car on the open interstate. It took only seven hours for the landscape to break into the pastel-colored hills and buttes Aurea saw in her dream.

"This is it," she said, her hand on the window as if she needed to touch the horizon to make it real. She looked out at the beautiful scenery but instead of the happiness she usually felt here, she felt pensive as her sense of dread grew worse. Just how big was this area? She pulled out her phone and searched for information.

The national park alone was more than one hundred square miles, to say nothing of all the land outside of the park that fit the image Aurea saw. She was overwhelmed with the immensity of it. As she looked for more information on the area, a headline appeared in the search results: Body found at National Park.

She gasped out loud before she could stop herself. Panic blurred her vision. *Don't let it be Adam.*

"What is it?" Thomas's voice was soft.

Aurea skimmed the article before answering. She let out a breath as she read the description in the first paragraph.

"The body of a woman was found at an overlook this morning," she said as she looked over at Thomas. His grip tightened on the steering wheel and his jaw muscles flexed.

"Do they know who she is?" he asked.

"It doesn't look like it. She didn't have any identification on her," Aurea answered.

"Do *you* know who she is?"

Aurea sighed and answered truthfully. "Maybe. I can't be certain, but yes, she could be the woman who called me. There's no way this is a coincidence. Jackson is involved."

The thought was devastating. They already knew Jackson was a kidnapper and a lunatic. Now they knew without a doubt that he was capable of murder.

"The area where she was found is closed for the investigation. We can't go there." Aurea read through more of the article. "The rest of the park is open, though. We should go take a look."

Thomas didn't respond. Aurea saw his angry expression fall into one of defeat. She understood completely. If the woman was dead, how did they even know if Adam was alive? Even if he was alive, the chances were slim that he was still in the same spot. Jackson wouldn't have gone through all this effort to make it this easy for them. He also wouldn't go through all this just to end it so early. Adam must still be alive.

"Follow the signs to the park. Let's get as close as we can to where she was found."

As Thomas drove, Aurea pieced together everything she knew about Jackson. Regrettably, it wasn't much. He grew up wealthy and privileged and now had the job of his dreams. At least, that's what he said in his fundraising speeches. He wanted to help children who did not grow up with privilege achieve their dreams in science. Though she always felt a darkness in Jackson, she, like everyone else, believed he meant it. She now felt foolish and naïve. She should have seen through his rhetoric.

He was wealthy and privileged. That part was true. He clearly didn't have the best interests of children in mind, so why was he raising money for science research and education? More pressing, who is the woman he killed and why is she dead?

Aurea had no answers.

She looked out the window as Thomas drove slowly around the gentle twists and turns. The view was breathtaking; Miles of buttes and valleys, the same pastel colors she saw in her dream, stretched out in every direction. The sky was bright blue today, with large patches of white clouds that drifted in front of the sun. She saw a herd of bison in the distance. It was an unneeded reminder that though it may look peaceful and beautiful, there was plenty of danger here. And Adam may be out there.

Thomas's voice pulled her from her thoughts.

"Do you see anything?" he asked.

"No. Let's stop and get out for a while."

Thomas parked at the next overlook and Aurea hurried out of the car. She walked to the edge and gazed out at the horizon.

"I don't think he's here," she finally said.

"He has to be here."

As she stood there, Aurea started to understand her opponent. Science truly was his dream job, and this was just more of his research.

"This isn't where he's taking us. This was a litmus test," she said as much to herself as to Thomas. "It's like I said before. He has a bigger challenge for us, but first, he wanted to see if we were worth the effort."

"Well, we're here. How do we let him know?" Anger was creeping into Thomas's voice.

Aurea went on the defensive. "I don't know. You talked to him last."

"Yes, but you seem to know an awful lot about Jackson and what he's doing," Thomas said as he turned to Aurea, his face flushed with rage. "Are you in on this? Are you working with him?"

Aurea was taken aback by the accusation and Thomas's sudden vehemence. First, it scared her, then the fear turned to fury.

"Are you kidding me? I have done all of this to find Adam and now you're accusing me of being part of it?" Aurea balled her hands into fists but kept them at her side. "I don't even know you and I'm risking my life to save that child. I know things because I pay attention. It wouldn't hurt you to open your eyes to the world now and then."

"What does that mean?" Thomas's voice was loud. "I'm not some crazy, free-loving psychic, so I can't possibly know what's going on?"

Aurea's anger swelled to a peak. They stared at each other as she took several deep breaths to calm herself before speaking.

"I don't care if you think I'm crazy, but I've never claimed to be psychic," she said. "And didn't Christ himself believe that love should be freely given?"

Aurea walked away toward the car and past it. She didn't care if he left her there. *I'd rather walk home to Minnesota than get in the car with that jackass.* She walked for a solid five minutes without looking back. Once she finally cooled off, she slowed her pace and heard rough steps on the road behind her. She stood very still as panic coursed through her. There were a lot of wild animals out here. She turned slowly to face whatever followed her.

"I was worried you'd come upon one of those buffalos." Thomas stood 20 feet behind her. His face was still red, but he looked embarrassed rather than angry.

"They're bison out here," she said to him.

"I don't know the difference."

"Me neither, now that I think of it." Aurea let the tension drop out of her as she walked back toward her brother.

"I'm sorry," he said to her. The two words carried the nearly tangible weight of guilt and sincerity. "I struggle with my temper and sometimes I just lose it."

Aurea made herself soften. "Me, too. I think we get that from our father."

They walked quietly the few minutes it took to get back to the overlook. As they approached, Aurea noticed something she hadn't seen before. It was on the asphalt of the parking area, just over the side of the cement curb.

"Thomas, do you see that?"

"No, what?"

"Hidden on this side of the curb. Is that a toy?"

They hurried to the curb where Thomas kneeled down and picked up the small toy car. He held it tightly in both hands like he didn't want to look too closely at it. After a moment, he opened his hands and turned it over. A name was written in permanent marker.

Adam.

"It's his." Thomas's voice was a raspy whisper. "He was here."

Adam

Adam hugged his backpack to his chest. All that he had left of home was inside. A few pencils, the clothes he was wearing when he went to school, a collection of superhero figurines, and his favorite book.

"Sir, may I please read my book?" Adam asked. His mother would probably fall over dead from surprise if she heard him being so polite. He knew how to be polite; he just didn't normally remember to do it.

The kidnapper kept driving as he gave his permission. Adam had strange feelings when Mr. Cole complimented him on wanting to read. He hated the man, but he was happy to please him.

For some reason, Susan left in the middle of the night. She didn't even tell Adam goodbye. He was afraid he did something wrong and she no longer wanted to help him. *She found out,* he thought.

When they first stopped in the park yesterday, they let Adam play outside. He rolled his toy cars along the curb by the motorhome while Mr. Cole and Susan talked. It sounded like an argument. A few minutes later, Mr. Cole wanted to find a different spot to rest for a while. As Adam picked up his toys, he held his favorite in his hand—the bright red Ford Mustang. His father bought it for him, and Adam loved it so much he put his name on it so it wouldn't get mixed up when he played with his friends.

"Dad will bring you back to me," he whispered to the toy as if to reassure it. He checked to make sure no one could see him, then tucked the little car behind the curb.

Now, he worried that Susan saw him after all and went back to get the car. Maybe Mr. Cole didn't want to wait for her, so he left. Or maybe Susan had changed her mind about helping him. Adam wondered what he had done wrong. *Why did she leave me?* He was now completely on his own.

Too anxious and sad to read, he opened his book and stared blankly at the pages. He read the story about the boy and his dragon so many times, he had it memorized. He let himself fall into a daydream about a dragon landing in the middle of the road so Adam could run out and climb on his back to fly away. Mr. Cole couldn't follow because the dragon would breathe fire at him. Along the way home, they would stop and pick up his dad and Aurea. Adam knew they were looking for him.

He didn't know how he knew, but he did. It was the only thought that comforted him. Right now, Adam needed all the comfort he could find. At the last town, Mr. Cole stopped at a store for some supplies, and Adam didn't like the looks of them at all.

Chapter 9

Jack stood behind his wife's chair with his hands on her shoulders. It took him hours to convince her that their son was delusional in the idea that Jack had other children, and tragically, those delusions led to the kidnapping. Nothing was proven to the contrary, so that was the only story allowed in the house. Now, the agents were back and told them about a body that was found in a national park in North Dakota.

"I don't see what this has to do with Jackson. The body was hundreds of miles from where Jackson is," Patricia Cole said. At 68 years old, she was a force to be reckoned with. She exercised every morning and finished every evening with Scotch, straight up. What she did in between, Jack didn't know. He assumed it was something to do with her charities or women's clubs.

"Mrs. Cole, the woman has been identified as Susan Brown. She worked with your son, and she was the child's school counselor." Jack felt his wife's shoulders twitch beneath his hands as the agent continued. "This is a murder investigation now, in addition to the boy who is still missing. We need to know if either of you has had any contact with Jackson."

"I've tried to call him several times, but it just goes to voicemail," Jack told them. "His mailbox is full. I can't even leave a message. What else do you know about this woman?"

The second agent replied, "Nothing else is released at this time. I'm afraid that's all we can tell you."

Patricia and Jack agreed to let the agents know if Jackson contacted them in any way, then politely escorted them to the door. Once they were gone, Patricia went to the bedroom to lay down. Jack went to his study to work through the new information.

A body was now linked to Jackson. That would intensify the investigation and there was no more keeping this out of the media. It was time to control the narrative. He called his public relations head for an emergency meeting. He then poured himself a drink a cursed his son for doing something rash and reckless and leaving it for Jack to fix.

It wasn't the first time. Jack had been covering for Jackson for most of the boy's life and it seemed the problems kept getting bigger.

Can't get much bigger than murder, Jack thought. *But if it can, Jackson will find a way to do it.*

Western North Dakota

Thomas knew he had to eat. His body demanded it, but his will would not cooperate. His plate sat full and a glance across the table showed him Aurea was having the same problem. He wondered if he looked as beaten down as she did. It was only three in the afternoon and they were both exhausted. With no idea about where to head next, they checked into the only hotel near the national park but had to wait another hour before they could head to their rooms. The attached restaurant seemed like a good option.

They were miserable.

Thomas had renewed hope after finding Adam's toy Mustang. His wife sobbed when he called and told her. It made him ache to be with her, to comfort her. He knew comfort would only come when he and Adam were heading home.

He just didn't know how to make that happen.

He looked over at Aurea again. He regretted his early outburst, but she still raised suspicions in him. He knew very little about her. They talked during their drive over the last two days, but it was awkward. They were two strangers and two very different people. How could he possibly know if she was telling the truth? He was being asked to blindly trust everything she said. If he didn't, Adam would pay for it. Thomas couldn't refuse, but he also couldn't go all-in. He was prepared to do whatever he had to do to get his son home.

At the moment that meant eating some food to keep up his strength, and so he did.

Two hours later he was in his hotel room, clean, somewhat rested, and anxious to get back on the road. He talked with his wife on the phone and then with his dad. Their voices gave him strength and calmed him enough that he was able to fall into a deep sleep for several hours. It was late at night when Thomas awoke again. With nothing else to do, he turned on the television and found the local news starting. The top story was the body found at the overlook.

"Authorities are not releasing the identity of the woman whose body was found earlier today at Theodore Roosevelt National Park," the anchor read into the camera. There was very little other information, so he turned off the television and checked the status of his phone on the charger.

Half-charged battery, no new notifications.

That's exactly how he felt, too.

He decided on a walk to pass some time. The air outside was bordering on cold, so he pulled on his light coat. The small tourist town was quiet, even the restaurant and bar were already shuttered for the night. He imagined since the tourist season was over there wasn't much of a late-night crowd. The entire town seemed asleep, except for a single person about a block ahead walking toward him. In the dim light, he could just make out Aurea's face.

"I guess we had the same idea," he said as they met.

"Yeah, sometimes being outside helps clear my mind."

Thomas couldn't handle small talk. "Any idea what we do next?"

Aurea took a deep breath. "Not yet," she said.

He just nodded. *I'm starting to lose faith in you,* he thought. He hoped it didn't show on his face. Being a doctor, he had years of experience in keeping his thoughts out of his expressions.

"I'm going to go back. I'll see you in the morning." Aurea seemed uneasy talking to him. She headed back toward the hotel and Thomas continued around the block as he organized his thoughts.

I'm losing faith in Aurea. Did I have faith in her? That's ridiculous. We're not to have faith in people, only God. What verse is it? From the Psalms: 'When I am afraid, I put my trust in you.' God, I'm afraid. I'm putting my trust in you. You'll show us where to go next. You'll guard Adam and keep him safe.

What happens to the people God doesn't keep safe?

No. God has always kept Adam safe. He brought Adam to me and made me a father.

He didn't keep my mother safe.

But that was God's will. Who am I to question God's will?

What if it's God's will that Adam doesn't make it through this?

Stop. Just stop.

The conflicting thoughts volleyed through his mind in a powerful mental beating. He was exhausted again by the time he made it back to his room. Thomas decided he needed some real rest and took a prescription sleeping pill. If they had to leave early, Aurea would have to drive.

That's okay. She needs to do something useful.
Stop.

Across the hall, Aurea sat cross-legged on the bed with her eyes closed.

I open myself to information and ask the record keepers to show me what I need to know.

Thoughts materialized and dissolved with no particular rhythm. It took her many months to learn the skill of making her mind open to information. Focusing on a thought is much easier than trying to keep them all out. She allowed thoughts to come in naturally, acknowledged them, and then dismissed them. Her mind was open until the next one came in.

Her thoughts tonight centered around Thomas. She sensed he was unhappy with her. She hadn't built up trust with him as she hoped. He was fighting an inner battle that perhaps even went beyond Adam's abduction. The light she associated with Thomas was flickering. She experienced this feeling before but didn't realize the flickering was coming from Thomas. She thought it was her own abilities dropping out, not his light weakening. Now she was certain that he fought his own flashes of shadows.

Of course he does. He's only human. But how much darkness is he fighting?

Aurea let herself focus on those thoughts for a few minutes, then pushed them out of her mind.

I open myself to information and I ask my record keeper to show me what I need to know.

She waited in the blackness of her mind for a long while before an image started to form.

A baby's cradle is bathed in light. Inside it, a baby cries. It's Adam. She's certain it's Adam. But why is she seeing him as a baby? Where is he now?

The image fades as another forms.

Thomas holds Adam, who is now a toddler, and reads him a book.

Aurea's mind is black once again. She waits patiently as the next image takes its time materializing. Her heart seems to flutter as she realizes this image is now.

Adam is laying down, asleep with a book in his hand. She sees inside his dream, where she stands with him.

"I know you're coming for me," he says.

"Yes, but I need you to tell me where you are."

"I don't know. It's so dark here." His voice is on the brink of terror. "I'm afraid of the dark."

"I know you are. It won't be dark for long," she reassures him. "Adam, where are you?"

He starts to fade.

"Adam, we're coming to take you home."

"Promise?"

"Yes, I promise."

Aurea kept her eyes closed as her mind awakened. She realized that she was laying down and had fallen asleep.

Her instincts told her she wasn't safe. Someone was in the room with her. She opened her eyes and moved to sit up but just inches in front of her was another face, that of a young girl. Aurea startled but couldn't move. Her stomach turned as she smelled peppermint and something much worse, something rotting. Aurea's breathing was fast, too fast, and all her senses seemed sharp. She could see too much and hear too much. She had to get away, but she couldn't. The girl was too close, and Aurea couldn't force her own arms up to push her away. She leaned over Aurea's face, and Aurea gagged from the odor of her. Her blonde hair fell forward as she leaned and swept over Aurea's skin. That's when Aurea saw it wasn't blonde at all. It was grey and brittle and the girl was old, with grey skin that hung off her bones. The rotting smell was thick and heavy and Aurea tried not to breathe it in. She closed her eyes and turned her head, then felt cold hands on her throat and sensed the movement of her own hair as the grey-skinned woman leaned close to her face and whispered in her ear.

"You can't have him."

Aurea forced her eyes open again and the woman was gone. She lay on the bed, afraid to move.

I was still dreaming. It was a nightmare, she told herself. *But it was so real.*

She slowly got out of bed, afraid that a hand would reach out from underneath it and grab her leg.

That's ridiculous.

She walked into the bathroom and turned on the light. In the mirror, she noticed her hair was a mess like she'd been tossing around in her sleep. She left the bathroom light on as she walked back to the bed, then decided to turn the main light on as well, for good measure. She went back to the bed, got under the blanket, and stared at the ceiling.

"I'm too old to be scared like this," she said out loud. Still, it took her nearly another hour to relax enough to get some sleep.

Even with both lights on, she failed to notice the strands of hair that had fallen to the floor. They were neither blonde nor grey. They were amber.

Rapid City, South Dakota

The ringing phone irritated him. Adam was sleeping, and as much as Jackson didn't worry about the quality of his sleep, he couldn't stand for the kid to wake up and start crying again. He grabbed the cell phone and answered the call before it could make more noise. He didn't speak until he was outside.

"What?" Only one person had the number. He knew who was on the other end.

"That was foolish, to let Susan's body be found so easily. You should have hidden it better."

Jackson bristled at the critique. "It was by design, a reward for following the clues so well. Like giving a mouse a treat when it finishes a maze correctly."

"How is this a reward?"

"It's information. Susan's body was my guarantee that the path is correct. It was needed."

"That's fine, but you've opened yourself up to more problems. We have more to clean up."

"Now is not the time to worry about that. Tomorrow is a big day. Things will change in the morning."

After they said goodbye and ended the call, Jackson wondered how many more times he would have to explain himself. This was his project, even though he required some extra help. He was in charge, and he was tired of having to answer to other people. His frustration boiled as he thought about it. He wanted to savor his excitement over his experiment finally happening, but now, she had taken some of that excitement from him. One day, he would be free from her neurosis.

He reminded himself that until then, she was helping to financially support his research. She was very interested in finding answers about life after death, and she respected Jackson's scientific approach.

By the next morning, the frustration had all but disappeared as Jackson prepared himself for scientific observation. The key, he knew, was to eliminate all emotion. Human emotion had no place in observation; it would pollute the results. It wasn't an issue for Jackson. He was never what one might call 'sentimental.'

His mind already worked over the steps he had to take that day as he gave Adam a simple breakfast of strawberry Pop-Tarts that Susan had brought along, and then prepared the motorhome for a drive. It was just after dawn when they headed out on the final stretch of their trip. It wouldn't be long now.

Chapter 10

They were headed into the mountains. That much Adam knew. The road curved and there were a lot of trees. After they left the city campground that morning, Mr. Cole made a stop on the mountain road.

"There's something I want you to see," he told Adam. They stood on the side of the road and looked at a mountain that had faces carved into it. "That's Mount Rushmore. I want you to remember it."

It must be part of the test, Adam thought as he did his best to memorize the faces.

The morning glow in the sky started to turn a cold fall gray as they continued. Drizzly rain patted onto the windshield. It made Adam nervous for some reason, but he couldn't figure out why. He watched the clock on the radio on the dash. It was 7:05 when they stopped to look at the mountain. It was now 7:48 and Mr. Cole hadn't said another word to him yet. He just kept driving. Adam quietly watched the numbers continue to change. At 8:06, Adam spotted a sign made of large rocks piled on top of one another. At the top stood a metal figure that made Adam shiver. It was the same monster animal that stared at him on the road two evenings ago. The words painted on the rocks were just visible through the dreary haze: Custer State Park.

Mr. Cole turned the motorhome onto the park road. It was smaller than the last one and had more bumps. Adam watched the trees pass by and wondered what other kinds of animals were out there, other than the one on the sign. He was worried that he would be finding out. He was tired of traveling on the mountain roads but was still hoping Mr. Cole wouldn't stop and park. He didn't want to go outside. He closed his eyes and silently begged Mr. Cole not to stop.

It didn't work. After curving through a maze of roads, each one worse than the one before, Mr. Cole pulled the motorhome into a small spot that was hidden in the trees.

Adam felt sick to his stomach.

Mr. Cole got up and walked over to Adam. He didn't say a word as he picked up Adam's backpack and started putting things inside: a flashlight, a big bottle of water, something small and shiny that Adam didn't recognize, and several granola bars. With each item, Adam's stomach felt worse.

"Okay, Adam, the rain has stopped. It's time to begin. Get your coat," Mr. Cole told him.

Adam stayed silent as he put on his coat and followed Mr. Cole into the rain outside. He had a hard time making his body breathe and each breath came out in short blasts of air. His heart pounded in his chest so hard he could hear it in his ears. The inside of his body was blazing hot, but his skin felt icy. Sweat trickled down his back. The edges of his vision darkened and blurred, and his mind was fuzzy. He couldn't hold a thought in his head, except that he was going to die. He was certain of it. Mr. Cole was going to kill him.

"Adam, what did we stop and look at earlier today?"

Adam's voice stuck in his throat.

"Adam, you need to concentrate now. You're in the test now and everything you do from now on will determine if you pass or fail. Now, what did we see earlier?"

"Mount Rushmore?" Adam was surprised the words made it out.

"Yes, good. We're going to go for a walk now. Pay attention to the things you see."

Adam only nodded.

Mr. Cole didn't say another word as he put on a backpack of his own and headed out into the forest. Adam walked fast to keep up. He still wore the sweatpants Susan gave him and he had to stop occasionally to pull them up. He tried to see everything he could, but everything looked the same. Each tree looked like every other tree; each hill looked like every other hill. At times, he heard sounds coming from the dark spots between the trees. After a while, he looked back and couldn't see the motorhome, or even make out the path they walked that should trail behind him. If something happened to Mr. Cole, he wouldn't be able to make it back. He hated Mr. Cole, but he hoped nothing happened to him.

About the time Adam's stomach started grumbling and his legs felt like they couldn't walk anymore, Mr. Cole decided to stop for lunch. They had been walking for hours. Adam was an active kid, but he had never walked so much in his life. He was happy for the break and to see that Mr. Cole brought a blanket and some food in his backpack.

"Here, Adam. I need you to put this on," Mr. Cole said to him. He handed Adam a strange-looking hat. "Turn around and let me adjust it."

Adam did as he was told and jumped as he felt a pinprick on his scalp.

"Turn around and look at me. Pay close attention," Mr. Cole said with a very serious tone. "You have to always wear this hat now until I take it off. If you take it off without me, it could short circuit and hurt you very badly. If you leave it alone it will be fine, but never take it off, okay?"

Adam nodded. He sat very still, afraid to set off the bomb that had just been placed on his head.

"You can move like normal. Nothing's going to happen. Just make sure you don't take it off."

Adam felt only a little better as he ate an apple and a sandwich and drank some orange juice that tasted a little weird but was still refreshing. His body was exhausted from the long hike and after he ate, his mind grew exhausted, too. With blurry eyes, he saw Mr. Cole speaking to him.

"You take a rest. When you wake up, you just start telling your dad and Aurea where to find you. That's all you have to do."

Adam tried to fight the sleep that was coming, but it was too strong. He needed to stay awake to keep Mr. Cole from leaving, but he couldn't keep his eyes open. He knew he would be alone when he woke up. His instinct was to panic again, but his body wouldn't even do that. He fell back on the blanket and let the darkness take over his mind.

4 P.M.
Aurea

It was the exact view she had in her mind. That morning, images of Mount Rushmore came into her dreams. She slept later than she intended, but she was grateful for it. She didn't know how well she could connect with Adam while she was awake. Now, after nearly five hours in the car, she and Thomas stood at a scenic stop where they could see Mount Rushmore from afar.

"Are you sure this is right?" Thomas asked.

"Yes. This was in my dream. I've never seen it before."

"Where do we go from here?"

Aurea swept her gaze over the mountain peaks on the horizon. Adam was out there somewhere, but 'somewhere' was a very large place. How could she possibly know where to go? She opened the car door and sat in the passenger seat. "I need to think for a few minutes."

Thomas watched her through the window. She could feel his eyes on her. Several times that day she had noticed him watching her, evaluating her. He was waiting for a miracle, and she had none to give. All of her insights and intuitions felt useless, insignificant, even reckless at this point. She had no way of telling if they were on the right track. No wonder Thomas was skeptical of her. She really didn't know what she was doing.

Still, she did get them to the Badlands. She was the one who found Adam's car. Thomas would still be in San Francisco and no closer to saving Adam if she wasn't there.

She closed her eyes and pressed her back into the seat in a stretch.

"Are you going to sleep again?" Thomas asked as he sat in the driver's seat. Aurea heard an accusation in his voice. It irritated her.

"No, just trying to see what we've missed." Aurea organized her thoughts into words. "We need to consider who it is we're working with here. I read some things on the internet about Jackson while you were driving, trying to figure out what resources he has or who he's working with."

"And?"

"Well, he seems to always stick to the script. All the public comments I saw from him, the fundraising speeches, the comments on the research, it all seems very uniform. He doesn't do things on the fly. All of this had to be very well planned out, and I'm certain he stuck to the plan every step of the way." Aurea paused to collect more of her thoughts. She continued, speaking more to herself than to Thomas. "That means some of the assumptions I've made were wrong. I thought the woman who called me was turning on Jackson, finding someone to come and help Adam. But that wasn't it. I was dumb to miss it."

"It was a part of his plan from the beginning," Aurea rubbed her forehead as she continued. "Even though we're so close to my home, to where I started, he needed me to work with you from the beginning. I had to go to San Francisco and get you so you would be part of this goose hunt, too. Jackson wants you and I both to be here."

"Why?" Thomas asked. Aurea noticed he sounded more intrigued than angry now. "He was torturing me just as much when I was home with my wife."

"Yes, why do you need to be here? That's an important question. Do you not want to be here looking for Adam?" It was Aurea's turn to make the accusations.

"Of course I do." Now Thomas was mad. "What are you insinuating?"

"Nothing. I'm just working through the process. Jackson is smart, calculating, careful. None of this is by accident. But one thing keeps sticking out to me. He's not an original thinker. I don't know a lot of scientists, but it seems to me that to make great discoveries, you have to have a big imagination. You have to wonder what's possible."

"Jackson's never made any discoveries," Thomas interjected. "I saw that when I looked him up earlier."

"No. He's fixated on this one idea, that somehow human consciousness can see everything. And if it can see everything, it can somehow control everything. He's using my connection to Adam to somehow prove that. But how is he using you? You don't seem to have the connection. You don't believe in it." The next words tumbled out before Aurea could stop them. "You're not even Adam's biological father."

Thomas was as still as stone. Aurea wished desperately she could pull those words back in but they hung heavy in the air between the two of them. She braced for another of his outbursts.

Instead, his voice was calm and even.

"How do you know that?" he asked.

Aurea didn't want to answer. She flashed scenarios in her mind.

"Tell me how you know that."

"I told you, I knew about you for a long time. I wanted to know who you were. There were court records."

"You looked into my court records? There really is something wrong with you." Thomas's face was flushed. Now, the anger was coming. "What else do you know about me?"

"Nothing. That's all I know. I just wanted to know who my brother was," Aurea heard herself pleading.

"Get out of my car."

Aurea hesitated for only a moment. Thomas opened his door and got out. Aurea followed and stood watching as Thomas took her bag from the trunk and dropped it on the ground. He didn't look at her as he got back into the car, started it up, and drove away.

Aurea stood on the side of the road. She knew he would not be coming back for her. She was on her own. It should have been that way from the beginning. Now that she was free of Thomas, she could get to work.

Adam

Adam woke up slowly, feeling the cold seeping into his body from the ground. He lay with his eyes closed, afraid of what he would see should he open them. At the sudden sound of a footstep on his left, his eyes blinked and opened. His head turned. A tawney brown doe stood a few feet away. It startled and ran off. Sudden panic flashed through Adam, and he grasped the top of his head. He was relieved to find the weird hat still there. He sat up carefully so it wouldn't fall off.

Adam looked around. He was alone. Panic crept up once again.

Jackson

He watched the deer sniff around Adam. Maybe he should have picked up the food before leaving to find his perch. It didn't matter now. Jackson was to have no contact with the boy now. He saw Adam awaken with a small movement that scared the deer off. Now that the boy was awake, Jackson's observation was underway.

He was tucked back in the woods, far enough away that the boy wouldn't likely spot him. Jackson carried powerful binoculars to watch what he could. He had also attached a small camera to the boy's backpack. As long as Jackson could find a cell signal, he could access the feed. It was all recorded to a file in the camera, so even without a cell signal, Jackson would be able to view the footage later. Now he would wait and see what happened.

Thomas

His tight grip on the steering wheel made Thomas's hands cramp. He had driven that way for miles, his mind full of curses and profanities against Aurea and Jackson. He wondered what else he didn't know about them.

Thomas and Amanda had never hidden the fact that Adam was adopted. It didn't matter to them. He was as much their son as if he shared their blood. They had been trying to adopt for years, but it hadn't worked out yet. *In God's timing*, they told each other often. And then, God's timing happened. A woman selected them to be the parents of her child. They never met the woman, but they continued to pray for her. She gave the boy the name Adam, and out of respect for the birth mother, Thomas and Amanda kept it. Thomas always knew he could love an adopted child as his own because his father loved him that way. The adoption wasn't some shameful secret, but it infuriated him that Aurea knew about it. She had been stalking his family. And he welcomed her into his home.

"I never should have trusted her," he said to the empty car. He drove forward, simply because that was the way the car was pointed. She was the compass and now she was gone. "I shouldn't have left her."

A turnoff and a sign were up ahead. *There must be a town up here eventually*, he thought. He slowed down a little and read the words *Custer State Park* as he drove past the turnoff.

Chapter 11

If you get lost, just stay in one spot. Adam remembered his mother telling him that when they went to the fair. It would be better to be lost at the fair. There were a lot of people around to help him.

Here, there was no one.

He sat cross-legged on the ground and held on to his backpack. He had already repacked Mr. Cole's backpack with the blanket and the leftover food. It worried him that Mr. Cole left his backpack. Maybe he didn't leave Adam alone. Maybe something took him. Maybe it would come back for Adam.

I know that didn't happen. He left me. Just like Susan left me.

It was too much to process and so he stopped trying. He thought about the things Mr. Cole had told him over the last few days. He needed to remember everything he saw and find a way to show it to Aurea. He looked around the forest and knew it was too big to try to remember everything.

When you have a big task, just break it down into bite-sized bits. That was from his teacher, Mr. Grafton. Adam looked around again and wondered how he could break down the forest into pieces. He decided to start with the tree nearest him.

He sat at the base of the tree and looked at the bark around the trunk. From this close, he could see it was many shades of brown. The bark was filled with cracks and lines and was rough to the touch. He looked up the length of the tree and saw it was taller than his house. It looked like a giant, skinny Christmas tree. He closed his eyes and pictured in his mind everything he just noticed. He tried to create an image of it that was exact to what he saw with his eyes. As he imagined the tree, he opened his eyes to check his progress or to look again at something he couldn't remember. *Are the pine needles dark green or light green? How far up was the first branch?* When he was satisfied that he had the right image of the tree, he opened his eyes and looked at it again. He had done a good job. The only problem was, there were thousands of trees that all looked the same. How would seeing this tree help anyone find him? He had to figure out something else to show to Aurea. He had to go someplace that wasn't just trees.

Adam stood up and put on his backpack. He picked up the other backpack and put it on over his chest. He felt protected with it there. He was covered front and back. It was a heavy load, but it would be dark soon and he wanted all the protection he could get as he set out.

Aurea

Plenty of people stopped to see the view. A few glanced over at Aurea and quickly looked away so as to not make eye contact. Once, she thought the person may talk to her, maybe ask what she was doing there on the side of the road with no car, or if she needed help. She wasn't sure how she would answer. Mostly, the other travelers ignored her.

She was sitting on her duffle bag, looking out over South Dakota's Black Hills, as she had been for the last hour. Panic and indecision crippled her. She held out hope that Thomas would come back to get her, but in her gut, she knew he wouldn't. She called the only person she could think of, and ended up leaving a rambling voice mail before hanging up, and giving up. For the last hour, she ran scenarios through her mind. Would someone offer her a ride? What if law enforcement showed up? How would she explain all this without sounding crazy? Would she find Adam before something terrible happened?

Her pulse quickened as the questions rolled over in her mind. She was sweating, though the air was cool. Trapped in her thoughts and worry, she jumped when someone gently placed a hand on her shoulder.

"What are you doing out here?"

Relief overwhelmed Aurea when she saw the familiar face. She stood up and grasped the woman in a long, firm hug.

"I didn't think you got my message," she said, her face buried in Nan's shoulder.

"I did. I've been trying to call you back, but it goes straight to voice mail. It's hard to get a signal up here sometimes." Nan pulled Aurea out of the hug to look her in the eyes. "What in the world is going on? Your message sounded frantic."

"I don't even know where to start. It's so … It sounds so crazy."

"Well, let's start with some food and water. You look like you've been out here a while. I have some camp chairs and supplies in the back of my truck."

Aurea picked up her bag and followed Nan to her parked truck.

"This should be more comfortable than the ground," Nan said as she unfolded the chair for Aurea. She set up a second chair for herself and took out an ice chest before sitting down. "I was leading an educational tour up the hill, but I was nearly all the way back down in Rapid City when I got your voicemail. I probably passed you on the way down and didn't know it."

Aurea watched as Nan set up the little lunch camp for them right there on the side of the road like it was the most natural thing in the world.

"I hope you eat turkey," Nan said as she handed Aurea a paper bag. "That's all I have left for sandwiches. Eat some, and then we can figure out your situation. Answers come better on a full stomach."

Aurea hadn't noticed how hungry she was, but her stomach growled loudly at the appearance of food. She ate the sandwich and drank the bottle of water the Nan provided.

Neither spoke until they were finished. Then, Aurea started a timid explanation of her last few days. She watched Nan's expression register various degrees of surprise and questioning.

"I know how it all sounds," she said as she finished. She searched for understanding in Nan's face, but couldn't read the expression she held. Aurea felt a sinking sensation in her stomach and stared down at her shoes with disappointment and embarrassment. She had told the truth and hidden nothing, and now this woman was surely judging her, just like the people did back in California when they judged her mom.

"Tell me about your mother." Nan's question surprised Aurea. Had Nan heard her thoughts? Aurea decided to continue to be painfully truthful.

"She died in a house fire years ago," Aurea's gaze was distant with the memory, her voice heavy. "I didn't save her."

"How could you?"

"I'd been dreaming about it, but I didn't understand the dreams. They were too blurry. I didn't believe them." She had never spoken the words out loud and now she told a woman she barely knew. Her voice lowered to a whisper, "I never warned her."

Silence lingered between them before Nan gave a gentle nod and spoke again. "I understand. How could you trust something you don't believe?"

Aurea felt the weight of the question on her. She didn't have an answer.

"Where are you headed now?"

"I don't know. I don't know where to start."

"Do you need to call the sheriff? I can take you down where there's better service."

"Thank you, but they already know. There are a lot of people searching for Adam, but I think he's here."

"Why's that?"

"I saw it in my dreams."

"And you trust them this time?"

"I don't know. It's all probably a mistake."

Nan was thoughtful again for a moment. She settled in her chair with a far-off look in her eye. Aurea waited for her to speak.

"My name, Nahimana, means 'secret' in Lakota. There are many secrets I know. There are a lot of secrets in these hills. That mountain over there," she pointed to Mount Rushmore in the distance, "is *Tunkasila Sakpe Paha*, the Six Grandfathers. It is sacred to the Lakota people. Long before politicians commissioned that carving for the sake of tourists, my people revered it as a place for prayer and devotion.

"The Six Grandfathers mark the six directions: North, South, East, West, above, and below," Nan continued. "They carry love, understanding, wisdom, and vision. They are seated in the Black Hills, which is a place of healing. I don't think it's a mistake that you're here."

Aurea had turned her back on what her mother believed and in the end that meant she ignored the opportunity to save her mother. What signs had she been ignoring lately? How much time had her disbelief taken from Adam?

"Where do I go now?" she asked.

"You tell me. I'll take you wherever you need."

Aurea trusted her gut. "I need to keep going on this road. I don't know to where."

"Okay, let's pack up."

"You'll help me?"

"Of course." She seemed surprised at the question. "There's a lost child out there. What kind of person wouldn't help?"

Custer, South Dakota

Thomas found a hotel with a brand name he recognized and got a room for the evening. The small town was about fifteen miles from the state park sign he saw earlier. He decided he needed a place to stop and regroup. He ran out of anger about halfway there but still made the decision not to go back for Aurea. There were too many unanswered questions, and he didn't know who to trust.

His wife had called him while he drove earlier and left a voice mail. He listened to it, but there was no new information. He wanted to call Amanda back, but he wasn't ready to tell her that he left Aurea. What would he say to her? What would she say to him? He looked up a number for the only other person he could think of and dialed it.

He hung up on the first ring. What was he thinking, calling Jack Cole out of the blue like that? What would he say? It wasn't like Cole would answer the phone himself, though. A receptionist or someone would answer and take a message. He could just leave his name and number. Satisfied with his plan, Thomas dialed the number again and gave his information to the person who answered. He told her it was a family matter, and the doctor would understand when he got the message.

He nearly choked on the word 'family'. He still wasn't sure he believed that Dr. Jack Cole was his biological father, but even if he was, that did not make him family.

That done, now the only thing he thought to do was wait.

Waiting was torture. He needed to do something. He opened the browser on his cell phone and started searching for information on the local area. He was looking for a logical solution to where Jackson may have taken Adam, though he didn't know how logical things were at this point. He sat down on the bed and glanced over at the bedside table where a local travel brochure had the headline *Lose Yourself in Custer State Park*. The image of the sign he drove past earlier flashed in his mind. How did he possibly miss it?

He grabbed his coat and his keys and nearly ran out to his car. He had to get back there.

The car was silent, but thoughts filled Thomas's head with noise. He again battled the barrage of accusations and doubts, and his normal tricks of controlling them were not working.

Why did I leave her? She was the only connection I had to Adam. Adam's going to die now and it's my fault.

Don't do this to yourself. It's not your fault. She overstepped. She shouldn't have talked to you like that.

How am I going to find them in this giant forest? This is hopeless.

Stop.

He turned at the state park sign and stopped at the visitor's center to get a map of the park. Stretched out over more than a hundred square miles, there were several campgrounds and a maze of roads. The feeling of hopelessness threatened to overtake him as he returned to his car. He sat in the driver's seat to look over the map and try to logically decide where he would go if he wanted to hide.

Unfortunately, every spot on the map seemed to match that description.

He didn't think it would be so easy as turning down the first road, and it wouldn't be by any of the lodges or education center. Jackson would probably have wanted to get away from other people as quickly as possible, so Thomas decided to take the first road that looked deserted. It wasn't exactly a logical plan, but it was a plan.

Thomas thought about the timeline and how long it had been since he last saw his son. It was only a couple of days, but it felt like weeks. Jackson said Adam would be on his own. *How long ago did Jackson drop him off? What supplies did he have?* The questions swelled up around Thomas again. *Have I taught him enough about survival?*

What about you? What do you know about survival? What do you know about being a father? Not enough to keep your child protected, obviously.

Arlington, VA.

Jack looked at the message with contempt. Thomas Hernandez actually called his office and left a message. Jack felt the world starting to crumble beneath him. This was all going to come down on him, and all because of Jackson's rashness. Jack poured himself a whiskey and sat at his desk. His wife's musical voice floated down the hall as she led the agents back to his study. They should know the way by now, Jack thought. He put the message in the top drawer of his desk and decided he would deal with it later when he was alone.

"What's the latest?" he asked as the agents walked in.

"We're looking for any previous connection Jackson may have had to the family of the missing boy. His father works at a hospital in San Francisco. We believe you may be on their donor's list. We'd like to see if you have records of donations."

"Who's being investigated here? Is it only my son, or are we under scrutiny, too?" Jack felt warm under the collar.

"You're not being investigated at this time, but it would help us understand Jackson's motive if we can piece together what he knew about the Hernandez family."

"My wife would know where to find all that. She's meticulous with our records." Jack tried to brush off any suspicion. "I think the hospital was her idea. Something about pediatric work."

Jack wondered how much she really knew about the reasoning behind his many donations. She always praised him for being generous as he donated to hospitals and scholarship funds. Every time he upset her with one of his angry outbursts, he opened his checkbook and sent money off to some new cause she supported. Some of those causes served Jack very well, like money to the science foundation that resulted in a good job for their son. One day after Jack threw a vase across the room in a fit of anger over something his wife said, he apologized by committing to a series of donations to a hospital in San Francisco that was on the cutting edge of treating children with genetic disorders.

"I also donate to starving children in China or someplace, so make sure you ask her for that, too." Jack's temper was beginning to boil over. He needed to calm himself before he let slip that private part of his personality. "I'm sorry. I'm sure you can understand how difficult this all is for our family."

He showed the agents back out and sat again at his desk. He stared ahead, not looking at anything in particular, but seeing the threads of his life starting to unravel. He wouldn't have that. He had to take some action to get control of the situation. A name came to mind, and he picked up his phone.

Jackson

Jackson rarely second-guessed himself. His preparation was always meticulous, and his plans were carried out without surprises. Still, this time, he wondered if he didn't overlook a key component: He was the one stuck out in the woods observing the subject. He was not a fan of the outdoors. Jackson wished a research assistant could take his place, but there was only one who would follow his instructions in this extreme of a situation, and he already killed her.

Some would say Jackson was raised wanting for nothing. He went to the finest schools, had the finest clothes, took the finest vacations. But that was just the public persona, built to match the public images of his parents. In reality, even at the finest schools, he was picked on by bullies who thought he was strange. He'd stain his fine clothes by being careless with his science sets – or just by eating dinner – and have to face his father's temper. His parents went on fine vacations while he stayed home. It wasn't accurate to say he wanted for nothing. As a child, he wanted for plenty of things: friends, affection, to feel included. As he grew, he replaced friends with high-level books on Einstein's quantum theories, affection with the ability to turn off all emotion, and inclusion with a deep desire to prove his superiority over those who ignored him his entire life.

Now, here he was, watching a child touch a tree like it was the first time he ever saw one. Jackson wrote down notes, stating the subject seemed to be practicing conscious observation of his surroundings. Jackson's interest was piqued when the subject put on both backpacks. It seemed he was preparing to make a move. What would come next, Jackson wondered.

Jackson took careful steps as he followed far behind his subject. Fortunately, the boy was also moving slowly. Jackson was certain he remained unaware that he was being followed. Jackson would only follow on foot for as far as a mile. If the subject traveled farther than that, Jackson would rely on the camera and its GPS signal to monitor where the boy was headed and what he was doing. Following him wasn't as important as observing how he was connecting with his surroundings. And even that wasn't as important as the end result of discovering if another person could find the subject solely through quantum telepathy.

Already, understanding of other quantum phenomena is proving beneficial and could lead to several applications. Quantum entanglement, the theory that two or more quantum particles can become linked and act as one, has led to work in quantum communications with a focus on better protecting digital data. The science community embraces such work. Jackson's area of quantum telepathy was still too mystical for most scientists. Jackson repeated that to himself every time he felt another scientist didn't appreciate his work.

I'll teach them to laugh at me, he thought.

The thought was enough to make him forget how much he disliked the outdoors. He had plenty of reasons to make this a success.

Arlington, VA

Jack appraised the man sitting across the desk from him. He wore an expensive blue suit and leather shoes. His short brown hair was meticulously styled with just the first few strands of gray showing, and his perfectly polished white teeth nearly sparkled above a strong jawline. It was no wonder this man did so well on television. He was the charismatic anchor on the national evening news, and one of Jack's longtime patients. They maintained a very good relationship, as Jack always kept the man's misgivings completely private. It was now time for him to return the favor.

"Thank you for coming in, Charles, and on such short notice," Jack said.

"Of course, Jack. You've always been available when I needed you."

"I have a situation that will be devastating to me once it's made public, even though I've done nothing to deserve it. I need your word that what I tell you now will be completely confidential, and when the time is right, you will have the exclusive." Jack waited for confirmation from Charles before continuing. Once he had it, he took a deep breath, folded his hands on his desk, and began. "My son has done something terrible."

Jack told Charles what he knew, omitting the mention of his own illegal medical research decades earlier, and saving the family connection for the last.

"Jackson believes the boy's father is my illegitimate son. There's no substance to that, and I'm afraid it's more of Jackson's disturbed thinking." Jack hesitated, unsure if his next words were right. He decided it was the best way to spin the situation and continued. "I'm afraid there's a history of criminal activity in my wife's family. It was so long ago, but one does wonder if these things somehow run in the bloodline. Of course, I didn't know when I married her.

Who's to say what I would have done. We were young and in love."

Jack let his voice trail off. He wasn't nearly as vulnerable as his words and tone implied, but he needed the sympathy of the nation's favorite news anchor. That would win him the sympathy of the nation. Let them hate Jackson for what he did. Jack would be the loving father who tried to help his son have a good, productive life but, alas, was unable.

"I can see you're taking it in. What do you suggest I do?" he asked.

"Well, you're right. This is going to be big when it hits the news," Charles replied. "I'm glad you came to me. We can work this out together. What if you made a plea to your son to return the boy unharmed?"

Jack felt a calmness wash over him for the first time since the ordeal began. He would be the one directing the narrative on this awful situation. He had found the way to take back control.

"When should I be at the studio?"

Chapter 12

"Why isn't this all over the news?"

Aurea thought about Nan's question as she watched the road stretch out ahead of them.

"I think it was, back in San Francisco," she said. "There was an emergency 'Amber Alert' that went out on the news and directly over millions of cell phones in the area, but it had already been several hours when Adam's parents found out he was missing. It was too late."

"What about Jackson? He really believes Adam can send thoughts to you?"

"Yes. He believes human minds can connect with each other, and that Adam and I can prove it."

"What do you believe?"

The question felt impossible. Aurea wasn't sure how to put her beliefs into words anymore. Even during the time when she had turned her back on her mother's teaching, she still knew she had it within her. She still trusted her instincts and intuition, but she switched off the full power of it. The memory of that time filled her with instant guilt. She had been so foolish and wasteful of the time she had with her mother. The thought put a lump in her throat, as it did every time it came to mind.

Now that she had returned to what her mother taught her, she practiced meditation every day and listened for what the universe was telling her. She was living her life at peace, but she realized now that she never fully let that power back in. She still kept a bit of it blocked, like she was still trying to subdue herself in order to fit in.

Or, she realized now, she was blocked by the guilt. She could never give in to the energy completely. Every time she tried, the guilt was there, strangling her. And it would always be that way. The guilt was so closely tied to her memories of her mother, if she let go of it, she'd lose a part of that connection. So, she clung to it tightly and wasn't willing to give it up, no matter how it damaged her.

When she finally spoke, her voice was soft and broken and meant only for herself. "I believe everything she ever taught me."

Almost as she said it, Aurea's body tensed with the sudden need for movement. Her limbs felt agitated with energy, and she had a nearly uncontrollable need to open the door and jump out of the moving pickup truck. She fought to control it as she looked for a place to pull over.

"Take that road and pull over. Quickly!"

Nan turned and found a spot to park. As soon as the car was stopped, Aurea opened the door and got out. She jogged to the end of the asphalt and looked at the woods beyond.

"He's in there," she said as Nan approached. She knew it without a doubt.

"I'll go get a map," Nan said.

Aurea looked at the nearby building and the few people she could see through the windows. "Please don't tell anyone."

Nan nodded and headed to the building. Aurea returned her gaze to the woods. It looked like they went on for an eternity. She simply stood there and watched the trees until Nan returned with a couple of large bags.

"The ranger said we have about two hours of light left. I told her we wanted to go for a hike," Nan added in a hurry. "She pointed out a couple of trails and some camping spots. I also got us more water and some protein bars."

That was smart, Aurea thought. She thanked Nan and accepted one of the bags. As they walked back to the car, she wondered what else they would need. Nan already seemed much more prepared than Aurea did. Aurea didn't have time to be prepared. Everything had moved very quickly over the last few days.

In stark contrast to the whirlwind of the last 48 hours, Nan drove very slowly on the park road. Aurea rolled her window down to let in some fresh air and to feel closer to Adam. She did not feel a connection while in the car. She needed to get out and be in the forest.

"Can we find a place to park so we can walk for a while?" she asked.

Nan drove a few more minutes and found a public camping area. It was nearly deserted and near a trailhead. After they parked, Nan packed some items in the backpack she had in the truck from her earlier tour and Aurea got her coat out of her bag. She was already in jeans. Her sneakers weren't ideal for hiking, but they would have to do. Nan was properly dressed in jeans, a flannel, and hiking boots. They were all worn-in enough that Aurea could tell Nan wore them often. The thought was comforting.

Once ready, they walked several feet into the tree line.

"Which way should we go?" Nan asked.

Aurea shook her head. "I can't tell."

"Here, I'll show you something my grandmother showed me a long time ago."

Nan set her backpack on the ground and had Aurea do the same. She positioned herself so she and Aurea were standing next to each other, facing the same direction.

"You've lost your focus because you're focusing too hard. Look directly at a tree," she said. "You see that tree, and that's good, but your mind isn't letting in details about anything else around you. You see blurry blobs of colors, light, and shadows, but not the whole picture. Now, relax your focus. Without moving anything, even your eyes, see the trees over to both sides. See everything in front of you."

Aurea did as Nan instructed. She focused on a tree in front of her, then let her focus soften. It took some effort at first, but soon she started to notice things she hadn't spotted earlier. Included in the pine trees were other leafy trees with leaves in orange and yellow. There were small flowers that grew in patches on the ground. A squirrel ran up a tree far to the left as a bird fluttered around a tree far to the right. She was seeing it all happen at one time, though she was looking directly at none of it.

"You can see it all because you're not busy seeing only a piece," Nan explained. "That is how you can open your thoughts. Let go of that sharp focus you have on one or two thoughts and instead allow yourself to see all of them. That will allow the things you need to see to finally get through."

Aurea stood and tried to relax her mind as Nan said. It was much easier out here in the woods for her to feel connected to the energy around her.

"I see tree bark. The roughness of it. I'm alone, afraid. There are too many trees." Aurea waited, but nothing else came. "That's all."

"That's all for now," Nan said. "It's a solid start."

"Yes," Aurea put her hand on the tree in front of her. "He's out here."

Thomas

The forest was vast. Thomas looked at the trees and was frozen with indecision. He had driven several miles through the park and taken two side roads. He now was at a picnic site with no idea where to go next. As he sat on a bench, he tried to remember the last time he prayed. Had it been at the cathedral when he first met Aurea? He usually prayed every night at least, but the last few days had been anything but usual. He sat silently in his car and spoke to his God.

It was gentle and ritualistic at first as Thomas said the words he'd been saying since childhood.

"Our Father who art in Heaven, hallowed be thy name…"

Thomas's shoulders relaxed. Every word, every syllable was a comfort, warming him inside and calming his mind. He spoke slowly and embraced the impact of the words. It was the Lord's Prayer, the perfect way to speak to God, and he felt in his heart that God was listening.

"Lord, you tell us 'do not fear, for I am with you; do not be dismayed, for I am your God. I will strengthen you and help you; I will uphold you with my righteous right hand.' I'm asking you to help Adam. I believe all miracles are possible through you. I pray for you to provide a miracle." His hands trembled with the weight of his words. "Please lead me to Adam."

Faith and fear cannot exist together.

He opened his eyes in surprise as the thought came into his mind clear as day. Had his fear been pushing his faith out? There is no fear like the fear of losing a child. It was too big to handle. How could he let go of it and let his faith take over?

Your fear is not too big for God.

Thomas closed his eyes again, took several slow, deep breaths and repeated that sentence to himself. When he opened his eyes, he felt renewed and calm. He was ready to find his son, no matter what it took.

He went back to his car and dug around in the trunk as he gathered several items into a backpack. Once he was sure he had anything useful packed inside, he put the backpack on and locked the car. He would set out on foot from here.

He used the GPS and map on his cellphone to get a general idea of the direction he wanted to go, but he knew reception wouldn't last far into the woods. It was already weak at the clearing where he was parked. Just the same, he marked his car's location on the map so he could get back to it. To save on battery, he put his phone on power-saving mode. He didn't know what technology he may need later.

Thomas took in as much of the scenery as he could as he walked. It wasn't for sightseeing, but to look for any sign that Adam and Jackson had passed through. He was also memorizing landmarks to help him on his way back to the car. Years of being a doctor had taught him to look for anything unusual and use it to determine the next steps. He wasn't trying to diagnose a mysterious illness or label an injury but rather trying to decipher the mind of a madman. *The method is the same, however*, Thomas thought.

In another situation, the scenery would have been beautiful. Deep green Ponderosa pine trees stood tall and stately, offset by brilliant Aspen trees with their ghostly-white trunks and leaves in various shades of yellow and gold. Still more contrast, the wide leaf canopies of the elm trees, with their rough, dark brown bark and orange leaves just starting to turn red. The forest floor was carpeted with leaves of various colors and shapes, the dirt in between still damp from the earlier mist. Everywhere he looked, there was color and life.

But there was no sign of Adam.

He would walk the entire forest if he had to. His son was out there, and he was going to find him.

Adam

Noise keeps bears away. Adam remembered that from a cub scout outing when they went camping in the mountains. His dad went with him, and they sang songs as they walked to scare off any bears along the path. Adam sang the songs again now and walked as loudly as he could. He didn't want to become bear food. He had no idea what time it was or how long he had been walking. He only knew the shadows in the trees were getting bigger. He wasn't hungry yet, so he figured it must not be too late in the evening. He decided to keep walking until he couldn't see anymore.

Another trick he learned from his dad as they hiked in the woods was to stop every so often and look behind him. That way, if he walked back in that direction, it would be familiar to him. It wasn't helping much because everything looked the same in the trees. As he looked behind him this time, he thought he saw something move in the distance.

"Hello?" he called out. "I'm lost. I need help!"

He waited to see if anyone answered him. There were only the sounds of the woods. The sounds frightened him. That was another reason he sang, to drown out the noises of the leaves blowing or animals walking around. They scared him badly. Adam wanted his mom. She always made him feel better when he was scared.

His stomach ached with loneliness and terror as he fought off the urge to curl up on the ground and cry. It wouldn't get him any closer to home if he stopped walking. So, he continued, although he couldn't stop the crying.

The strange hat was tight on his head and made his skin itch. He reached up and scratched around it, but the hat shifted slightly and he felt another jab in his scalp. He froze in place and prepared for something bad to happen. After a few seconds of nothing, he decided it was safe to continue walking.

A tree limb cracked in the trees to his right.

Adam's heart felt like it would explode from fear.

Something moved.

Adam's legs started before he had time to think. They propelled him forward and ran for his life. The backpack over his chest beat into his face with each step. He put a hand to his head to make sure his hat didn't fall off. Everything was a blur. He wanted to look back to see what monster was behind him, but he didn't dare. He dodged around trees and ignored the scrapes against his pants from the brush. His vision was blurry, and he didn't see the obstacle until it was too late.

Adam tried to jump over the fallen tree, but he didn't jump in time. His leg hit the tree and he fell over it, face and arms first, to the ground. Pain blinded him for a long moment, then fear set in.

His hat was gone.

He couldn't move.

This is where he would die.

Adam closed his eyes and thought about his mom. He formed a picture of her hugging him and tucking him into bed. She sang to him. He told her it was angelic. His dad said it was okay to give compliments even if it wasn't true. He wanted nothing but to hear that voice right now. As he concentrated on it, he started to hear it.

"Keep going," he heard his mother's voice whisper.

"Okay." Adam pushed himself up to a sitting position. It was a difficult feat while wearing two backpacks. As he got up, he saw a hole in the front backpack where a large twig had impaled it. It would have stabbed him if he hadn't been wearing the bag.

He brushed leaves and dirt off his arms and looked at the scrapes that bled through his shirt. His sweatpants from Susan were ripped and his legs bled. Though he was alone, he was embarrassed to realize he had wet his pants. He didn't know if it was when he was running or when he fell. For a brief second, he was glad there was no one around. He took both backpacks off and went through the one that was his to find his jeans inside. He changed his clothes and decided to leave the sweatpants there at the fallen tree. He never wanted to see them again.

Now that his panic was gone, Adam was ready to continue walking. His right ankle was swelling up and hurt with every step, but he had to keep going. Instead of running through the trees, his steps were slow and careful. The slow pace, the pain, and the growing darkness made him feel like everything was hopeless.

His mother told him once when things seem hopeless, look for the light.

He calmed himself and looked around. Ahead and to his left, there was a bright spot in the woods. The dark trees ended and the forest opened up. Adam stumbled and limped and rushed as much as he could, injured and overloaded with the backpacks, desperate to get out of the woods.

Aurea

All of Aurea's senses were alive. The sun was low on the horizon and brilliant white as it wove its way into the forest between trees and leaves. Her skin tingled with the touch of the cooling air. Everywhere she looked, trees big and small surrounded her like giant sentries guarding the woods. The forest floor was hidden by brush and fallen leaves in reds and oranges that looked like a sea of flames spreading out in every direction. Hanging in the air, the heavy scent of wet dirt and old leaves mixed with the freshness of the evergreens was so encompassing, she could even taste it softly on her tongue. The quiet of the forest was loud with the sounds of nature. A squirrel scurried up a tree, birds fluttered in the leaves overhead, a deer stepped through brush nearby.

To her, there was no place as wonderful as a forest, but she could only imagine how terrifying it would be to here alone as a young child. She pushed away her thoughts of worry and found a spot on a fallen tree where she could sit for a few minutes. Nan walked through the trees nearby looking for any sign that someone had recently passed through. They walked separately but within viewing distance of each other, so they could cover more ground. Aurea gave a small wave as Nan glanced over to her and signaled that she was going to sit for a few minutes.

She closed her eyes and breathed in deeply the scented air. She used slow, deep breaths to relax her body as she cleared her mind. By removing the visual stimulation, she let herself focus on what else her body was experiencing. The sounds were louder, the air cooler. With those sensations at their highest, she slowly opened her eyes. First, light came through her lashes, then blurs of color. As the blur became clearer, she kept her focus wide and her mind relaxed. With her eyes open, seeing everything but nothing, her ears hearing sounds that blended together, smell and taste combining as one, she felt connected to everything around her. She existed with all of it inside the Akashic field. She sat motionlessly and simply let herself be available.

The thought formed.

It wasn't something she saw or felt. It was something she knew, another bit of the Akashic records revealed to her.

In a snap, the trees in front of her were clear again as her vision sharpened into focus. She glanced over where she had last seen Nan but didn't spot her.

"Nan?" she called out.

"I'm here."

Aurea jumped as the voice came from surprisingly close. Nan sat on the ground a few feet behind her.

"I didn't want to disturb you," she said. "You were zoned out for 20 minutes."

"Thank you for not leaving me," Aurea replied. "Do you have the park map?"

"Of course." Nan pulled the folded map out of her jacket pocket and handed it to Aurea.

Aurea unfolded it on the ground between them. "We need to find a clearing. A big one, surrounded by the woods."

"That doesn't narrow it down very much."

"Something with running water nearby."

"Here," Nan pointed to a spot on the map. "There's a creek and a clearing. It would be a long walk from here. We should go back to the truck and drive over to that campground close to it."

"Alright," Aurea agreed. She folded the map and put it in her pocket as they started the twenty-minute hike back to the car. Aurea glanced at the sun through the trees. It glowed golden now as it crept closer to the Earth.

They wouldn't make it to Adam before dark.

Chapter 13

Jackson was tired from his walk back to the motorhome, but he had a lot of work to do. The first order of business was to move the vehicle to the nearby campground where it would blend in with the other motorhomes. After a few minutes, he was parked and sat at the small kitchen table with his phone in hand. He hated to call and check in, but he had a responsibility to the person who was paying for this excursion. Unfortunately, his news wasn't good, but he didn't plan to share those details. He dialed and didn't bother with a greeting once the phone was answered.

"The experiment is underway. I'm monitoring remotely," he said.

"Very good, son. What are you finding?"

"Heightened brain activity. It's going as I predicted."

"Very good."

"I am still waiting on a final piece of data. So far, no one has shown up to find him."

"How long will you wait?"

"I'll wait here for twenty-four hours. After that, I'll head to the safe house and monitor the news. They'll report if a missing child is found out in the woods."

"That is very smart. I knew you could handle this. But, be careful, Jackson. And remember, you're going to be the biggest name in…" The call became muffled for a moment and Jackson could hear some moving around. "I need to go. I may have a situation here."

Jackson finished the call and hung up. He had a situation as well. He looked at the laptop screen in front of him, at the flat lines he had been watching. If the device was recording brain activity, the lines would be moving. They stopped a half-hour ago. The GPS tracker he had placed in the backpack stopped at the same time. It was very likely Adam was dead, a victim of an animal attack or a bad fall. Jackson looked out the window. The sun was setting now. He'd have to go look for the boy's body in the morning.

As he watched the sun outside, a pickup truck pulled into the campground and parked in a spot near him. Shock and delight flashed in Jackson as he recognized the passenger. It was Aurea. She made it. Adam had called her to him from thousands of miles away. Jackson had hypothesized this would happen, but he could hardly believe the proof that was in front of his eyes. He had many questions for Aurea about her experience over the last three days. He couldn't let her get away.

He also couldn't let her know he was there. He watched through the window, ready to hide should she glance over. She never did. Her gaze was fixed on the trees in front of her. Her companion looked around, but Jackson was certain she hadn't seen him. He wondered how the other woman became involved. He had threatened Thomas not to get others involved, but it was an empty threat. Maybe they knew that.

That led to another question: Where is Thomas? Jackson didn't see anyone else in the truck. No other vehicles followed behind them. Did Thomas stay in California? Was there discourse between the siblings? He was curious, but it didn't matter. Not to the experiment, anyway. Aurea was the one he was studying. His partner would be mad that Thomas wasn't here, but he would deal with that later. Right now, all that mattered was Aurea.

He watched as the women walked into the wooded area and made the quick decision to follow them. The new person would make it hard for him to get to Aurea; he'd have to do something about her. First, he wanted to watch them and study Aurea as he had studied Adam for the short time he watched from afar. Jackson pulled on his coat and pocketed a small flashlight and a few other items. He watched from the window as the women walked into the trees. He paid close attention to the direction they took and watched until he could no longer see them. At that point, he set out to follow them.

He was confident they were unaware he followed them as they made no attempt to be quiet. He could hear the crunch of the leaves with every footfall. He kept his footsteps light and stayed hidden back in the shadows as he tracked the women. It was easy to blend into the woods, which were quickly being overcome by dark as the sun settled over the horizon. In addition, the women were very focused on what was in front of them. They paid no attention to what was behind.

Jack

"Be careful, Jackson."

Jack's mind was stuck in disbelief at what he just heard. He stood outside the door to his bedroom and listened to his wife on the phone. He pushed open the bedroom door, stunned by the thoughts he was putting together. His wife was Jackson's conspirator. The woman who was once a nurse in his office was a part of these disastrous events. He stammered as he searched for words.

"How could you?" was all he managed to get out.

Patricia's stare and voice were like ice. "How could I?" she asked. "How could you?"

"What?" Jack stammered.

Patricia stood up from where she sat at the edge of the bed and walked toward Jack. Her voice was low and level, the words slowly leaking out of her like venom.

"All those years, Jack. All those years, I was home while you traveled around. Did you think your naïve, sweet wife didn't know what went on when you were out? The clubs, the waitresses, the bottles of wine. I saw the receipts. I kept all our records." The ice in her stare turned to fire. Her words were slow and deliberate, her voice musky from years of burning anger. "Every time you nailed a stripper, I turned it into a tax write-off. How could you not realize that someday one of those girls would come looking for money? Who is the naïve one now, Jack?"

Jack could not process the new information. None of it made any sense. He sat on the edge of the bed and looked at his wife. There was a stranger in her body. He didn't know this woman. Finally, he asked the only thing that came to mind. "What did you do?"

"I made sure the world will be free of you. Jackson will be the last, and years from now when he dies, he'll take the last bit of your existence with him." Patricia's stare frightened Jack. "After years of your abuse, he was all too happy to help out."

"But a child. An innocent child?" Jack couldn't finish the thought.

"We were all innocent once," Patricia said with sadness in her voice. The sadness was for her own lost innocence, and not the child's. Jack was certain of it. Jack's chest ached with worry. Sweat beaded on his forehead as Patricia spoke again. "The child is the last of your heirs. He had to go. You're the one who caused this, Jack. You should have thought more about the consequences of your actions. Did you really think divorce was the worst you had to worry about?"

It was all too much for Jack. His head felt thick and his hearing turned muted like he was underwater. He felt pain rising in his chest and he struggled to breathe. The pain shot down his arm and he felt crushing pressure in his chest.

"Are you not feeling well?" Patricia asked with mock concern. "You should have that checked out."

Jack reached out for her. "Patricia, please."

Jack watched with blurry eyes as she walked out of the room. His head grew dizzy and his body slid off the bed. It seemed to happen in slow motion but there was nothing he could do to stop it. He landed on the floor with a thud, his limbs bent strangely beneath him. A figure formed out of the blur in his vision.

Patricia, you came back to help me, he thought. But it wasn't his wife's arms that reached for him. Grey skin peeled from the thin bones that came much too close to him. He smelled her decay as the cold fingers touched his throat. A small, gruesomely grey face came into focus as it leaned toward him. He knew who she was.

"Sarah." His voice was raspy. "Sarah, I'm sorry."

She sat inches from his face, her breath the odor of rotting fish as she replied.

"It's too late, doctor."

Thomas

Thomas walked quickly to make the most use of the remaining sun that he could. It would be very dark soon, and that would make everything worse. He walked along a stream in hopes that it would keep him from getting lost. The map showed him the stream ran for many miles within the park. Finding Adam would be a shot in the dark, and the dark was coming fast.

"Adam, are you out there?" His voice was growing tired from yelling every few minutes. He would yell until he had no voice left, and then he would yell anyway. He decided it was time to get the park rangers involved, but his cell phone had no service in the area, and he didn't want to waste time by walking an hour back to his car. He was now in a routine: Yell for Adam, check the phone reception, keep walking. And repeat.

As the light dimmed, his desperation grew. Every terrible scenario possible ran through his head: animal attack, terrible fall, freezing to death overnight. It never occurred to Thomas to worry about himself; he was too worried about his son for it to cross his mind that he, too, could die.

Yell for Adam. Check phone reception. Keep walking.

Aurea
There was no natural light left. Aurea pulled the flashlight from her pocket and turned it on. The beam of light seemed too weak for the woods, but it was something. From the corner of her eye, she saw Nan turn on her light as well. They panned their lights from side to side as they walked and looked for any trace that Adam or Jackson had been in the area. They'd been walking for more than an hour, and still no sign of either of them.

"How are you doing over there?" she asked Nan. They were walking close together now because of the darkness.

"I'm alright. How are you?"

"I feel like I'm supposed to feel helpless right now," Aurea said. "But I don't. I know we're on the right track."

Aurea walked like she was guided by something. She was sure of the direction she was headed. "I do need a little break, though. I have something in my shoe."

Aurea sat down on a fallen tree and took her shoe off. Nan sat next to her and scanned the area with her flashlight. A glint of something reflective caught the light.

"Did you see that?" Nan asked. She looked for it with the light again, jogged over to the area, and picked something up. "It looks like a hat. Ouch!"

She dropped the device and looked at her hand for a second before picking it back up again, more carefully this time. "That's weird. Someone stuck a thumbtack through the back and glued it there. It would poke a person in the head."

Nan walked over to Aurea and handed her the strange hat. Aurea took it and looked inside, hoping to find Adam's name as she and Thomas had on the car. She found something else.

"Are those electrodes?" she asked as she looked closer.

"I'm not sure, but it looks like it."

"Adam wore this. Jackson used the thumbtack in the back to scare him." Aurea handed the hat back to Nan. "We need to keep this. Can you put it in your backpack? We're close. Adam was right here and that was on his head."

Aurea scanned the area around them with the flashlight. She felt the strange sensation of someone watching from behind her, but when she turned around and shined the flashlight through the trees, she saw nothing unusual. Still, she felt it. Something was out there.

"We're close," she said, with only a little more confidence than she felt. "We need to hurry. We're almost there."

Aurea put her shoe back on as Nan put the hat in her bag. As they were leaving, Aurea thought she heard something in the woods behind her. It spooked her, but she tried not to show it. Whether from fear of what followed them or the hurry to find Adam, her step quickened even more. She felt it as real as she felt the air around her: Adam was nearby.

Adam

Dew was starting to collect on the grass. Adam sat with both hands on the ground next to him, fingers entwined in sharp, damp blades of native grass. He forced his eyes as wide open as they would go in an attempt to see as much as he could. The sun set an hour ago and robbed him of the safety of his sight. He couldn't see what else was in the trees, waiting to attack him. His breaths were deep and long, as he found earlier that the fast, short breaths of his panic caused too much noise and movement. Now, he imagined himself invisible. If he was invisible, nothing could hurt him.

A quick glance to his right told him the monsters were still there. They had moved in as the daylight ended, a herd of the eight or ten of the giant beasts. Adam hadn't moved once since he spotted them. He stayed, where he had sat down to rest, and prayed they wouldn't notice him there. So far, they seemed only interested in eating the grass and lying down to sleep. They were close enough that he could smell their dirty, musky stench, but they were far enough away that Adam wasn't sure they could see him. It wouldn't be so bad except they blocked the only path he could take that didn't involve going back into the woods. He was trapped.

Adam startled and turned to the left. He had heard a sound. What was it? A snap. A tree limb breaking on the ground far off in the woods. Then, someplace else, the howl of another animal. Surely it was a wolf coming to eat him for dinner. Or maybe something worse. What is worse than a wolf? Maybe a lion.

Fear pricked at his skin. His breaths came faster and shorter and beads of sweat formed on his brow. He didn't want to die here, in some strange place, alone and eaten by animals. He didn't want to die at all. He didn't know what would happen if he died. The church told him about Purgatory and Heaven. He didn't want to go to Purgatory, but he knew there were worse places.

The Nothing.

He shuddered at the words in his mind.

"Go to sleep."

Adam jumped at the sound of the voice. He looked around but saw no one in the darkness.

"Who's there?" he asked, his voice trembling and soft.

It was a girl who answered him. "Go to sleep so you can come play with me."

"Where are you?"

Adam stood and looked around again. The hairs on his arms stood up straight and a cold chill gave him bumps on the back of his neck. An electric pulse of fear raged through him and made everything in the woods seem louder. His breath came in puffs of white mist in front of his mouth and nose as he breathed short, fast gulps of air that made his mind dizzy.

A twig snapped to his right.

He turned but could only see the dark outline of the trees.

Another sound from behind him.

Adam circled around, both arms held out to protect him from whatever was hunting him in the darkness. As he searched, the girl called to him again.

"Go into the trees. I'll wait for you there."

He was scared, but somehow, he wanted to do what she asked. His feet wanted to lead him into the trees. Adam looked over to his right and saw the herd of beasts huddling with each other. He couldn't go that way. Behind him, there was nothing but deep darkness. He could either stay there in the clearing and wait to die, or he could follow the girl into the trees.

Into The Nothing.

He took a step toward the trees to his left.

Don't go.

It was a different voice. Maybe it was Adam's own, he didn't know, but it was loud and commanding. Maybe it was his father's. His father was supposed to always be there to protect him.

Why didn't he come find me? Why didn't they try harder?

It started as an accusation but turned into a deep sadness. Was he not good enough for anyone to come find him? Did he fail the test and now he would certainly die in these woods.

Adam missed his parents so much at that moment, he could almost hear his father's voice calling for him.

It only lasted a second.

The monsters far off to his right shifted. Had they noticed him sitting there? Maybe they smelled him the same way he could smell them. He was sure he smelled as bad as them by now. There was more movement. A different sound, this time from behind Adam. A new animal came out of the darkness with teeth so big they reflected the moonlight.

But, that wasn't right. Adam was confused. And then...

"Dad!" He screamed with every bit of might he had left in his little body. "Dad! I'm here!"

It wasn't moonlight reflecting off teeth that Adam saw. It was the weak glow of a flashlight about to lose its power. In the glow, he saw his father. He was there.

"Adam?" Was his father crying? Dads don't cry, do they? "Adam, don't move. Stay quiet. I'm coming to you."

His dad took very slow steps in Adam's direction, but he stayed turned toward the pack of monsters. They had noticed him, too, but so far, they hadn't moved. Time stood still for Adam. Was he imagining this? Would the monster get mad and kill his father right in front of him?

And then the worst happened. The biggest monster stood up and faced down his father. Its giant, hairy, horn-topped head swayed back and forth. Adam heard the beat of angry hooves stomping at the ground. It was going to charge his father.

Adam was just a little boy. What could he do to stop the beast from attacking his dad? He had nothing in his backpacks to help. His stomach was sick.

The beast started running. Others joined him.

The flashlight turned off.

Adam closed his eyes tight and covered his ears with his hand.

His father screamed.

The beasts snorted.

A strange loud sound erupted from the wrong side of the clearing. Another. Adam opened his eyes and looked toward the new sound. Two women were running across the clearing toward him. One held a gun and the other had a flashlight. The woman with the gun stopped and fired again into the ground. Adam quickly turned back to his dad but couldn't see him. The beasts stopped their charge and looked toward the women.

Two more gunshots.

The beasts turned and ran away from the sound. Away from his father. Away from Adam.

The woman with the flashlight reached him first. She ran to him and fell on her knees as she reached down to pick him up. She held him tightly and Adam held her back, both arms gripping as tight as possible. It was only a second later that he heard his father again.

"Adam!" His voice was so near. Then, he was there. His father grabbed him and the woman in a tight hug. "I'm so sorry. I'm so sorry."

The woman let go and it was just Adam and his dad. Adam buried his head in his dad's shoulder and wrapped his legs around his dad's waist. He wanted to be as close as possible, and he never wanted to let go.

The emotions were too much for the boy. The sudden relief of being found, of not being attacked, of his father being saved from the monsters, the fear of the dark woods, the terror of Mr. Cole and Susan disappearing and being kidnapped. It was too much.

The release came out as a long, full-body scream as Adam relived in one moment the horror of the last few days.

"That's okay," his dad said as he rubbed Adam's back. "Let it out, son. Let it all out. It's okay."

Adam screamed and he screamed again and again until it turned to sobs that shook his whole body and he cried out guttural sounds of an animal scared and in pain and screamed again, weak this time, as all the energy left his body. And then, protected in his father's arms, he let it all fade out as he fell asleep.

Chapter 14

Jackson watched from the darkness of the tree line. At first, he was angry with himself for letting the women slip away into the open, but then, he realized what was happening. He watched silently, amazed at the results of his experiment. The boy had not only led Aurea to his location, but also Thomas. Jackson had held no hope of Thomas having any ability to connect to the quantum consciousness. And still, here he was.

Jackson considered his next move. It would be harder to convince Aurea to go back with him now that she had more support. He had been ready to take the other woman out of the equation and quietly capture Aurea. Now there were just too many people. Plus, now he knew they had a gun. He's glad he didn't act too rashly earlier when he followed them in the woods.

Did he need to know what happened in Aurea's mind? He wanted to. He was curious; but did he really need to know for his experiment to be complete? No, he reasoned. The experiment was to see if the boy could direct another person to his location using only images from his mind. The boy did that. Jackson wanted to know how it worked, but that wasn't the goal for this experiment. This study was about *if*, not *how*. *If* was now proven. Jackson's next task was to document his findings.

To do that, he had to get out of there without anyone discovering him. He turned around and headed back into the deep blackness of the woods. He'd have to walk some distance in the dark before it was safe to turn his flashlight on. It didn't bother him much. His eyes had adjusted to the dark and he had a small pistol in his pocket. He walked quickly, knowing the boy could identify the motorhome in the parking lot. It was Jackson's only transportation. He needed to make it back to the campground and head out before the rest of them got out of the woods. Otherwise, he would be stuck hiding in the trees. He had a lot of very useful knowledge. None of it involved how to steal a car.

Thomas

"Here, will you check for a signal?" Thomas reluctantly let go of Adam with one arm as he handed his phone to Aurea. Adam stayed asleep. "I don't want to wake him. The last number I dialed is the emergency number for the park rangers."

"You called the park rangers?" Aurea sounded surprised.

"Yes. I told them we got separated while we were hiking. They're out looking for Adam," Thomas paused, "and you."

"Me?"

"Yes. I told them you and I split up to look for him. I was worried. It was horrible of me to leave you. I'm sorry." Thomas felt the weakness of the words, but he didn't know what else to say. He was embarrassed by his outburst that afternoon and felt relentlessly shameful for leaving her stranded on the side of the road. And after all that, she continued on until she found Adam and at the same time, saved Thomas's life. Any other person would have turned around and gone home. Or, more likely, any normal person never would have gone on this crazy chase in the first place.

He heard Aurea on the phone attempting to describe their surroundings. It was difficult with everything so dark. She hung up the phone and handed it back to Thomas. The next call he would make himself. He decided to wake Adam for this one.

"Adam, we're going to call mom so you can talk to her, okay?" He let his son wake up but continued to hold him tight as he called his wife. "Amanda, we have him. He's safe. Adam's safe."

Thomas was now the one overwhelmed with emotions. His wife's immediate sobs of relief set off other sounds Thomas could hear through the phone. Amanda's parents sounded nearby. He heard his own father shouting from across the room. Everyone wanted to know what was happening, why Amanda was breaking down. Thomas heard her tell them, her voice struggling against her own sobs. Thomas cried with her. He squeezed Adam tighter, then made himself relax and hand Adam the phone.

"Mommy?" Adam sounded even younger than he was. The trauma had taken a toll. He hadn't called Amanda mommy since preschool. Thomas wondered how long it would take for him to heal emotionally, if he would be able to at all.

Adam held the phone to his ear but didn't say much more than an occasional "okay" or "I love you, too." Thomas let him stay on the phone, silently listening to the quiet voice on the other end, knowing his mother was there. He would let him sleep with the phone next to his ear if he needed it.

As Adam had his phone call, the woman who came with Aurea got into her backpack and took out a pack of batteries. She put new batteries in Thomas's flashlight, then gathered all the flashlights they had between them and turned them on.

"The rangers need something to look for," she told Thomas. "I have more batteries if we need them, but it shouldn't be long."

It was about a half-hour later that they heard the hum of all-terrain vehicles. It was one of the best sounds Thomas had ever heard. His nightmare was almost over.

But there was a thought that lingered in the back of his mind, though he tried to silence it.

Jackson was still out there.

And he was dangerous.

Aurea

It was all quickly becoming a blur. There were moments when Aurea wondered if any of it actually happened at all. After the park rangers arrived, they got everyone out of the woods and to an office to answer questions. Adam was taken to the hospital for an assessment. He was in a state of shock, and had some minor cuts and bruises, but was otherwise unharmed. Physically, at least. His emotional health was another matter. It would take some time to heal from the trauma.

Thomas stayed with Adam at the hospital. Nan answered some questions, then was free to leave. She offered to stay with Aurea longer, but Aurea wouldn't have it. Their goodbye was awkward. What do you say to a near stranger who helps you through such an intense and emotional experience? Only when Nan was gone did Aurea admit the truth to herself. She wanted her to stay. It had been a long time since Aurea had a friend, and she could use one.

Now, twenty-four hours later, Aurea was awake early and ready to head to the airport for the short flight home. Thomas was on his way to pick her up at the hotel. He had slept at the hospital, unable to leave Adam's side for even a moment. Amanda was there with her husband and son. As soon as Adam was safe, she booked a flight to South Dakota so she could be with him. The family planned to drive home to San Francisco together. They would not be going through North Dakota this time, but Thomas told her that someday they would go back to the Badlands to heal. He didn't want such a beautiful place to hold bad memories. When they did, Aurea would meet them there for a visit. The thought made her smile. As she did, her phone rang. It was Nan.

"I'm sorry I didn't call yesterday. I slept all day," Nan said after they said their hellos.

"Me, too," Aurea replied.

"How are you doing?"

Aurea sighed. "Okay, I guess. It's all so confusing and frustrating."

"I saw the news coverage this morning. There's still no proof it was Jackson?"

"Nothing. Adam hasn't been able to identify him yet," Aurea said. "He's already had a full day to disappear, and police have nothing to go on."

Except for the voice recording, Aurea thought. The police wanted them to keep that detail private. Thomas recorded his conversation with Jackson when it all started. It couldn't be used to charge or convict Jackson because of wiretapping laws, but it was all they had. That, and Jackson's dead coworker, Susan, but unless he could be tied to the murder, it would be just a coincidence in the eyes of the court.

"How long are you staying in town?" Nan's question brought Aurea out of her thoughts.

"I leave this morning."

"I'll give you a call tomorrow to see how you're settling in at home if that's alright."

"I would like that." Aurea smiled, glad Nan couldn't see the flush on her cheeks.

She thought about it later as she rode in the car with Thomas. She knew none of them a week ago and now they were all connected to each other by this dramatic set of events, in addition to the blood connection she shared with Thomas and all it brought with it. She wondered how much she and Thomas were alike.

"Thomas, how did you know where to find Adam?" she asked.

"I prayed. I just kept praying and I was led there."

"I was led there, too. Sometimes I saw images, but sometimes I just knew where to go. Was it like that for you?"

"No," Thomas said. "I never saw anything. Never heard any voices or anything like that. I just felt it. If I was heading one way and started feeling anxious, I'd turn until I felt like I was going the right direction."

Aurea thought about the connection between her and her half-brothers. Thomas had his prayer, she had meditation, and Jackson had his quantum theories. In her mind, she imagined a triangle with each of their beliefs at a point. The points were all connected by common lines. It was like that with their beliefs: a common line ran through them. None were right, none were wrong. They were just three ways of traveling through the same space.

The pull seemed stronger for the three of them than for others. Thomas often saw his prayers answered. She lived her life with direction from her visions. Jackson was willing to kill to make others see what he saw in his science, and probably had. What had she missed in Jackson's personality? She and Thomas were relatively normal people. Or, at least, they didn't seem to have any psychotic tendencies. Thomas got a little angry now and then, but he saved people, he didn't hurt them. What had made Jackson so dangerous?

Washington, D.C.

As a person grows older, their perception of time changes. At ten years old, one year is one-tenth of your life. It seems a long time. When you're seventy, a year is only one-seventieth of your life. It comes and goes before you know it.

And so, it was. Patricia's life was flying by.

She looked at the pictures on the walls as she walked slowly down the hallway. They were not the happy family photos so many of her acquaintances displayed. These were neatly posed portraits with the subdued half-smiles of duty.

Forced.

Faked.

Just like everything else in the family. She married Jack so long ago out of duty. She had a family name to uphold and he was the selected suitor. She never complained, even back then. He was charming enough, handsome enough, respected enough. And she was ever dutiful.

She had hardly time to remove the wedding rice from her hair before Jack lost his charm and showed his true self. He was demanding and demeaning. He only got worse after the birth of their son.

He had been so proud when Patricia gave birth to a son. He acted like a medieval king who thought having a son was a display of his grandness, not a simple act of biology, and worse, that a male child was far more valuable than a female. It disgusted her. She was grateful she hadn't given birth to a girl. Who knows what the king would have done then.

Jackson was only in preschool when he started disappointing his father. Jack would throw great fits any time the boy acted out or made a mistake. Often, Jack didn't need a reason for his fits. He just felt like yelling.

Patricia protected Jackson as much as she could. Jackson didn't know the number of times his mother took the blame for something so that she would get the punishment instead of her child. Jack never laid a hand on his son; The same was not true for his wife. It was rare, but it happened. She never told a soul. Her husband was a prominent man, and her misery would be on public display. People from families like hers did not let that happen. Instead, she did her best to keep Jack mollified and to be the buffer between him and Jackson.

She wasn't surprised the first time she found out about one of Jackson's affairs. A woman knows when her husband is keeping secrets. Men think they're so good at it, but they give themselves away every chance they get. A woman can hear it in her husband's voice. Patricia learned that as a child when her own mother discovered her father's affair.

That's when Patricia's façade broke. It had been quiet for years, the demon inside her, the fury that made her bite a gash in her friend's arm when she wouldn't share a doll or poison a competitor so she'd have food sickness the night of the homecoming dance. She thought she had conquered it, all those times Jack raged on and she was wide-eyed and innocent, but it still burned inside her, an ember waiting to ignite a forest fire.

The fire was lit when she discovered a letter from a woman in California. She was expecting a child. A picture in the envelope showed a round-faced, blond woman sitting on the beach, her belly swollen with a child. A child who belonged to Patricia's husband.

Wrath fueled the fire, but Patricia was a smart woman. She didn't act out in rash bursts of anger. She always played the long game. She hired a lawyer, then wrote to the woman and explained the situation. She directed her lawyer to buy the woman a house as a payoff, in return for her never having contact with Jack again. It seemed fair to Patricia. She didn't blame the woman; certainly, she fell victim to Jack's charm just as everyone else did. She probably didn't even know he was married. Patricia wanted her and the child cared for, but out of their lives. The lawyer saw to it, and due to strict attorney-client privilege, not even Jack found out about the deal.

That was the story of Jack's daughter. Jackson was the one who discovered Jack had another son, just a few years younger than Jackson. He was gentle when he told his mother, as by this time she was already in her sixties and Jackson mistakenly thought his mother was getting frail. Patricia had little reaction to the information, but she did her research. She learned as much as she could about the man and decided to save the information for the right time. Little did she know the right time would come so soon afterward.

There was another pregnant girl. This time, Patricia was outraged. It came just after Jack turned sixty-one years old. The girl was in her twenties, young, scared, and stupid. She was finishing her degree and wasn't ready for the responsibility of a child. She came to Jack for help, but it was Patricia who opened the door. It took very little for the girl to come clean about everything. Jack was "sponsoring her scholarship" in return for her appreciative affection. Now, it seemed, her birth control failed.

That was the first time Patricia met Susan. She convinced Susan to end her relationship with Jack and to place the child up for adoption. Patricia knew a lovely couple in San Francisco that had been trying to adopt for years. If Susan made sure that couple got the child, Patricia would not only continue paying for Susan's science degree but would also make sure she had a job out of college as Jackson's assistant.

That was when the fire started to burn too hot.

Patricia's thoughts were consumed with the treachery Jack had brought into their home. She fixated on the need to teach him a lesson. She could think of little else. She had spent her life by his side so he could have everything he wanted. No more. She would take away the very thing that meant the most to him: his legacy.

Jack talked about legacy every chance he got. She was tired of hearing about it. Every time he started discussing it, whether with her or on stage at a grand fundraiser, she would stare blankly into his eyes and silently contradict every word. *You have no legacy, Jack. You've never done anything. Your son hates you. He won't continue your name. Your seed will end with him.*

Over and over, the words rolled in her head, until she could finally see it. She needed to end the evil of Jack Cole. She could only do that by making sure his seed did not survive. That would be difficult, but she knew she had help. Jackson would do anything to help his mother. Even more, he would do anything to hurt his father.

That's how the plan was born. Or rather, it was whispered in her ear one step at a time. If she thought about it, she'd realize she'd been hearing the whispers for a long time. At first, she ignored them, but they continued. They continued until she found herself whispering back. She had many conversations with the whispers.

You know where his notes are. I can't take them. *You already did. You made copies long ago. Leave the notes on Jackson's desk.*

Then, later: *Tell Jackson about the boy we found.*

And the loudest: *Empty the medicine into your husband's coffee.*

Patricia wished she could put a road map of that on her walls and display it as proudly as other women display their grandchildren. But no, it would stay her secret. That was how she protected Jackson. No one could know the truth.

She sighed as she thought about her son. He had made a few mistakes and things were more difficult now. Still, money could make anything work, and they had plenty of that. As far as she could tell, there was nothing linking Jackson to anything at this time. The phone call he made to Thomas was made from a cell phone bought under a fake name. It couldn't be tied to Jackson.

The biggest problem now was that all the witnesses were still alive. That's not how it was supposed to end. But Jackson was a smart boy. He always had a backup plan.

Adam

A thousand shades of orange speckled everything in front of him. Everywhere Adam turned, he saw a blur of orange. It frightened him. Then, it changed, as things do in dreams. The orange came into focus as the millions of leaves on the forest trees. He looked up and a shower of leaves floated down and brushed against his face with feather-soft strokes. He was no longer frightened. He was warm and happy. He felt safe here.

A voice spoke from his left, a woman's whisper. He couldn't tell what she was saying, and he looked but did not see a woman. Instead, he saw the leaves were now butterflies with brilliant orange wings. They fluttered around him, so thick a mass that he couldn't see through it. The voice whispered again. This time, he heard.

"Go to her."

He looked again, but no one was there. Then, as quickly as they came, the butterflies were gone. Adam was floating in water. It was cold and night was coming in around him. He felt the water inch up over his face and panicked as he realized he didn't know how to swim. He flailed his arms and kicked his feet as he tried to keep his face out of the water, but it did no good. The pull of the water slowly dragged him down. He watched as the surface moved further and further away. His panic faded as saw air bubbles floating away from his face and he realized he was breathing. He looked around for help and saw a figure floating in the deep water with him. Her hair floated all around her head in a golden halo. Her skin was white, her eyes were closed, and she had no air bubbles floating away from her face.

Adam reached out to touch her. As his finger brushed her icy skin, her eyes snapped open. Adam gasped in water and pulled his hand back. She spoke but he could not hear her. She was screaming, but no sound came out. Adam choked on the water and couldn't breathe. He closed his eyes tight and willed himself to wake up.

His eyes opened and he sat up in the hospital bed. His throat hurt as he said his first words since that scream in the forest.

"Aurea's in danger."

Chapter 15

The afternoon sun was subdued by the autumn haze as Aurea drove home from the airport. The northern Minnesota countryside was calm and beautiful, with soft rolling hills golden with the remnants of harvested cornfields or green from fields of grass that grew freely and held their color as long as possible before the winter struck. The serenity here was a welcome contradiction to the bizarre events of the last several days. Though she had slept well at the hotel, Aurea was still emotionally exhausted from it all. She let the silence in the car cover her like a warm blanket as she meandered through the countryside. She was eager to see her animals, though she was sure they had been well-tended by her neighbor. Still, she drove slowly to allow herself to come back to this reality and to shake the lingering feelings of anxiety she still carried. She didn't want to carry them home with her.

She had hoped to talk to Adam before she went home, but he was still in an unresponsive state of shock when she left. She had kissed his forehead and whispered in his ear that she would see him again and they would have a happy time together. She thought of that as she drove now. She would like to visit Adam sometime. She would even enjoy seeing Thomas again, if he would keep his temper under control. She hadn't quite forgiven him for deserting her on the side of the road, though she tried to keep in mind the extreme stress and emotions he was under at the time.

She pulled off the country road onto the long driveway to her home. The gravel under her tires was a welcome sound. Her dog, Sunny, greeted her at the door with a wagging tail and happy yips. Her cat held a grudge, as she did every time Aurea left, and glared with an arched back from her favorite spot in the kitchen. The food and water bowls were full, so the animals had not been neglected during her travels. She picked up Sunny and walked with him past a hallway and into the living room.

"He doesn't make a very good watchdog."

The voice startled Aurea. She didn't have time to turn around before he grabbed her from behind, pushed the dog away, and put a hand over her mouth and nose. Fear beat in her chest with heavy heartbeats. Her instinct was to run, but as she looked around, she didn't see an easy way out and Jackson was too strong. She tried to break his grip, but couldn't do it.

Aurea's panicked breathing was fast and each inhalation drew with it the sharp scent of chemicals. Her eyes burned from the fumes. She tried to kick her heels back into his shins, but her body was growing weak. Her vision blurred and her head grew dizzy. She tried to slow her breathing, to stop the hyperventilation, but even that didn't help. She tried to pull the hand away from her mouth and felt a cloth under Jackson's grip. He was poisoning her. It wasn't nearly as quick as it always seemed in the movies. Aurea held her breath, trying to will the chemical to dry out before she breathed again, but it was no use. She closed her eyes and fell asleep.

She was only out for a second, or so it seemed at first. But, that wasn't right. She passed out in her living room, and now she could feel everything moving. Aurea slowly opened her eyes, then blinked against the golden afternoon sun. She had not been out for long. She could tell by the sun and by the surroundings. She was in the passenger seat of Jackson's motorhome, and through the window, she could see that they were traveling down the same country road she had just left.

Her wrists were bound with plastic ties, but at least they were in front of her.

"Where are we going?" she asked.

"Not far. I just need to gather my final observations, and then we're done," Jackson said without taking his eyes off the road. "I saw a lake on the map that I thought would make a nice place to stop."

The answer didn't help Aurea much. They were in Minnesota, the Land of Ten Thousand Lakes, as it was known. The fact that the lake was on a map worried her. There were actually nearly twelve thousand lakes in Minnesota, and only the big lakes were on the maps. It would be more difficult for her to escape if he took her to a secluded area off one of the big lakes. That seemed to be exactly where he was headed.

She watched through the windshield as she quietly tried to unbuckle her seatbelt. She wanted to be able to jump out if she got the chance. She didn't know what she would do if she did jump out, but she'd have to worry about that if it happened. She watched for signs to see where they were headed, but it was little use. There weren't many signs on the rural roads, and she was still too new to the area to have explored it all.

Jackson drove along a gravel road that curved around the water. After he parked, he had Aurea move from the passenger seat to a kitchen table in the middle of the motorhome. He put a small recorder on the table and sat across from her. She placed her bound hands on the table and waited for him to speak.

"My research can't be complete until I find out about your experience with it," he said. "I need to know what it was like for you when Adam connected with you."

"This is insane. This isn't science, Jackson. This is," Aurea struggled for the right word, "demented."

"Yes, my technique has been unorthodox, but sometimes extremes are necessary," Jackson replied. "That's the problem with science in this era. Everyone is so afraid of public perception and staying within these arbitrary rules. Look what happens when we dare to break them. We can walk within the unimaginable."

Aurea was deeply afraid of Jackson. She had never seen a person fall into insanity, but she was certain she was watching it now. She stayed silent as Jackson continued.

"I've watched you for years, you know. I already knew you well when we met at that fundraiser years ago." Jackson raised an eyebrow and his expression transformed from wild to smug. "I even visited your mother's store. She told me what she believed in. She even offered to read my cards, not that I would let her. She was a nice woman, quite beautiful. It's a shame that space heater of hers was faulty. Burned the whole place down, or so I heard."

Aurea wasn't sure what she was hearing, but she ached inside. She had to know. "Did you start that fire?"

"It's really a shame that someone with such promise wasn't able to see that happening. It seems like one of you two fortune tellers should have known."

Aurea felt sick to her stomach. Despair welled up inside her like thick, black ink filling her from the middle out. It was heavy and sticky and it filled her. Then suddenly, it was rage and fire. She forced herself up, knocking the removable table off its leg and sending it crashing onto Jackson's lap. With her hands still bound in front of her, she pulled the metal table leg out of its socket on the floor, wielded it over her shoulder, and sent it crashing down to the side of Jackson's head.

But he was fast and not bound like she was. He pushed the table off his lap and threw an arm up in time to catch the brunt of Aurea's swing, but not all of it. The metal hit his raised arm and the side of his skull together, knocking him partially to the ground, partially splayed over the table that was now propped up awkwardly in the small space.

Aurea again swung the table leg as high as she could and brought it down against Jackson's shoulder. As she did, he reached up and grabbed a thick handful of her hair at the scalp and pulled her down to him. Off-balance and in pain, Aurea fell to the ground, her body added to the heap already there. The table leg was gone and her hands were still bound. A sharp pain flashed through her face as Jackson elbowed her. Blood welled up in her mouth and both eyes started to swell. Everything was a blur.

In an instant, Aurea switched from attack to survive. She swung her arms again, this time to find something to give her some leverage. She pushed herself away from Jackson, sliding on the floor. Jackson fumbled with the table as he tried to stand up. Aurea pushed herself to her feet and headed to the door. She stood up too fast and was overcome with dizziness. She leaned into the door as she tried to get it open but she wasn't fast enough. Jackson towered over her.

Through her blurry, swollen eyes, she could see the fury in his face. *He's going to kill me now.* There was not a doubt in her mind. She closed her eyes tight as he grabbed her hair again. He opened the door effortlessly and pulled her by the hair down the steps to the grass. This was her chance to get away. Blood dripped down her wrists to her hands. The plastic ties cut deep into her skin. The sting of the cuts was like fire on her wrists as she used her bound hands to push herself up. She tried to look around, to find anyone who could help her. Just as she realized there was no one, she felt another hard blow to her head. Jackson had kicked her.

She now laid on her side on the ground, blades of grass poking at the damaged skin of her lips and eyes. A blur of movement told her Jackson was coming at her again. She could do nothing to stop it.

The ground tore into her skin as Jackson pulled her by her bloody arms. *Where are we going*, she wondered with some delirium. A moment later, her question was answered as she started to sink in the frigid water of the lake.

"Mama," she whispered, "I'm coming. Wait for me."

Chapter 16

The small plane bumped with every cloud. Thomas wasn't fond of flying and this trip reminded him why. Aurea had flown through Minneapolis, Minnesota, a large airport with a lot of options and big planes. But none left from Rapid City, South Dakota, when he needed it. There was one flight to Grand Forks, North Dakota that left within minutes of him getting to the airport from the hospital. He bought a ticket, rushed through security, and made it onto the plane just before the doors closed.

It was the smallest plane he'd ever been on. It seated only twenty-four passengers and scarcely had room for the flight attendant. The only relief came when they announced there would be no drink service because the flight was too short.

Thomas spent most of the flight praying. He prayed for Aurea's safety, for guidance to find her, and that the turbulence would stop. He was filled with momentary relief when the plane landed without issue. He nearly ran to the only car rental company at the small airport and was outside in a car within minutes.

Grand Forks was right on the border of North Dakota and Minnesota, but it was a two-hour drive straight east to the address he had for Aurea's house. She lived in a very rural area near Red Lake, Minnesota, only about a hundred miles from the Canadian border. Thomas did the math in his head. He left only about an hour after Aurea did. According to the map on his phone, she had twice the drive from Minneapolis than he had from Grand Forks. When he added it up, he was less than an hour behind her now.

He tried to call her cell phone, but it went straight to voicemail, as it had the last fifteen times he tried to call. He had stopped leaving messages after the first five. He checked his speed, then pressed the gas pedal further down. There didn't seem to be any law enforcement around.

He wasn't entirely sure where to go, but Adam told him to look for water. The strangeness of the situation settled on Thomas. It used to be when Adam woke up crying, he and Amanda would comfort their son, tell him it was just a dream, and that everyone was safe. How quickly that changed. This time, he was out the door in minutes, on an airplane less than an hour later, and driving to an unknown location purely on the faith that this all had to mean something.

Faith. The word struck Thomas. His faith had certainly been tested lately, but he hadn't given up. He remembered words his mother told him once: Faith and fear cannot coexist. They cancel each other out.

There had been moments in the last few days when he was more afraid than he'd ever been in his life. In those moments, he acted rashly and nothing went right. When he slowed down and walked by faith, he was led where he needed to go.

"Trust in the Lord with all your heart, and lean not on your own understanding; in all your ways acknowledge Him, and He will make your paths straight," Thomas said the Bible verses aloud. It was from the book of Proverbs.

As he drove, he prayed for direction. And as he did in the woods, he listened to the directions he was given.

Jackson

Jackson watched Aurea float on the lake. He should have weighed her down, but she was too far out now and he was in no shape to go out into the water.

He never imagined she would fight as she did. Jackson's head screamed with blinding pain as he'd never felt before. His hearing was badly muffled and his eyesight was blurry. Thankfully, there was no one around to hear the sounds of their fight. He'd have to stay in the motorhome for a while until he recovered enough to drive. He limped his way from the lakeshore back to where he parked, using the fuzzy shapes of brown and orange trees to guide him.

As he drew closer, a new shape and color appeared. It was gray and black, maybe blue, standing tall like a person. Jackson blinked in an attempt to make the image clearer. It was a person standing in front of him, talking, asking questions that Jackson couldn't make out.

Jackson closed his eyes from exhaustion. Someone had found them. He would have to muster the strength to kill one more person. He didn't mind the killing; it meant nothing to him. At the moment that he stood there, slightly dazed, looking at the new person in front of him, Jackson remembered once again the first time he saw death. He had so many questions about it. What happened when a person died? What is it like in the collective consciousness? Is it empty?

But yet, it occurred to him that he never asked why that death happened. He was not yet a teenager, at work with his father, a doctor. His father wanted Jackson to see his work, so he would want to be a doctor just like his father was. But it backfired. A little girl died, his father said, for no reason at all. Jackson saw the body. He wasn't meant to, but he looked into the room as his father raced around and tried to bring the girl back.

Time escaped Jackson as he thought about it. Had it been a second? An hour? He didn't know. As he looked around, everything was the same. The blue/black blur still stood in front of him, talking. Jackson took a deep breath and gathered his strength. It was time to end this.

He rushed forward and used the element of surprise and his own body weight to push the person down. His hands found the man's neck. He held it with one hand as he punched with the other. Then, it all happened very quickly. The man shifted and rolled on top of Jackson. He was heavy on Jackson's weakened body. Jackson moved his arms around and patted the ground, searching for a weapon. He found a thick twig and gripped it like a knife as he pulled his arm around and stabbed the man in the neck.

It wasn't enough. Strong hands gripped tighter on his neck and squeezed away any hope he still had of surviving. Frantic thoughts flashed through his mind, vivid and colorful. Arms flailed in a weak final attempt to push the attacker's weight off him. He gripped at strong hands and looked into the killer's eyes. He saw no remorse, only the smug air of personal justice. And why not, he questioned silently. His last thought told him he probably had it coming.

Finally, he was consumed by the very emptiness that had terrified him his entire life.

It was dark in the void.

The Lake
"It's not time." Her voice was a faint whisper from the depths.

I'm tired.

"You'll rest soon." The voice was soothing, the warm comfort of undying love.

But I miss you.

"I'm right here. I'm always here. You have so much more to do."

I'm so sorry. The thought devastated Aurea. Three words packed with everything she wanted to say to her mother.

"I know. I know your struggles, then and now. You need to release them."

I can't. Again, the weight of the words meant everything. She couldn't yet forgive herself for not warning her mother about the fire. And she couldn't fight to stay alive any longer.

"Help is coming. Just keep floating."

Aurea lay still, afraid, and unable to move. The water that had been calm now bubbled and splashed around her. Her heartbeat quickened as a roaring sound filled her ears. She struggled to keep her body straight but remembered her childhood swimming lessons. Floating was a last resort if your body was tired, and you couldn't make it out of the water. Keep your face above water and lay still. Originally, she laid still so Jackson would think she was dead, then she laid still to keep her body above the water. She kept her mother's words in her head. *Just keep floating.*

She felt weightless on the water, but her body was tired. She started to bend in the middle as the water decided to finally take her. First her hips, then legs sank into the dark coldness. Her arms floated out to her sides as her torso drifted down, finally pulling her face so slowly under the water.

It only lasted a moment. Arms slid under her and pulled her back up to the golden sunlight of the surface. She drifted motionless as the arms pulled her along. Then, more arms reached for her. It hurt as they lifted her out of the water, so many hands grabbing her bruised and injured body. They held her and laid her on a hard, warm surface. She shivered and they covered her with a coat. They were talking to her, but she couldn't understand. There were too many voices, too many faces. Then one came close and moved into focus. She reached up and touched it.

"Thomas."

Her brother came for her.

Her family.

She closed her eyes again and let her body drift to sleep, knowing she was safe.

And loved.

Chapter 17

Over the weeks the winter rolled in, and cold darkness settled everywhere around Patricia. She had only the void, the emptiness. Her husband and son were both gone within days of each other. They were horrible days followed by horrible weeks of news reports and police investigations. Her husband died in their room from a heart attack, which people assumed was due to the stress of the situation. Patricia knew the truth. Her son was killed in a fight as another man tried to save a woman from a lake, a woman her son had tried to kill during an unhinged science experiment. Her son, a mad scientist.

She now lived cloaked in the pity of the people around her. She hated it. They pitied her for her loss, and they pitied her for the disgrace her son was in the end. They said he went insane, that he had become delusional because of his work.

Patricia knew the truth.

Her son was not insane, and he had protected her until the end. No one knew of her involvement in his research. Jackson had died with her secret. She had paid for it all. She had talked Susan into her role. She had told Jackson how to work the emotions of his half-siblings. Patricia had organized everything, and Jackson was the dutiful son.

When she grieved, she didn't grieve for the man people say went insane and became a murderer. She grieved for the man she knew Jackson to be, and she grieved for the little boy he once was. She grieved for the man who would do anything for his mother and she grieved for the child she always protected.

When she grieved for Jack, she grieved for the man he could have been instead of the one he was. She grieved for the years she wasted keeping up their public image and for a lifetime that could have been spent happy but wasn't.

Mostly, she grieved for the fact that there was no one left to grieve for her. In her desperate, deranged attempt to get revenge, to feel empowered, to feel loved, she had cursed herself to live in the dark aloneness of someone who had no one.

And that was how she died, only weeks after her husband and son, alone in the dark.

Sarah welcomed her into The Nothing.

San Francisco, Christmas

The city was alive with lights and colors and people hurrying around. Holiday decorations made the bustling city even more colorful than usual. Aurea indulged in the life of it all. The noisy crowds would have bothered her before, but now she reveled in them. Her near-death experience gave her a new appreciation for life and all the messiness that comes with it. Spending Christmas with her brother and his family in their busy, crowded city was exactly what she needed.

She still carried scars from her fight with Jackson. They all did. Thomas had a wound in his neck that was healing well. It was sheer luck that Jackson missed the carotid artery. Well, Aurea called it luck. Thomas called it a miracle.

Adam's scars were slower to heal, but his wounds were much deeper than the skin. Many nights a week, he woke screaming and crying, still trapped in the woods with monsters chasing him. He did alright when he was awake, but his new therapist was worried it would take a long time for the night terrors to go away.

Aurea thought about that as she squeezed the little boy's hand. They had just finished a trip to the movies together. Thomas and Amanda waited at home. It was a challenge for them to let Adam out of their sight, but they knew Aurea wouldn't let anything happen to their son. Nonetheless, they were waiting by the window as Aurea and Adam walked up the steps to the house.

"How was it?" Thomas asked.

"Great! We had a lot of fun," Aurea answered. "I bought him a lot of candy."

"You're turning into a fine aunt," Thomas laughed. "We have a surprise for you. Look who's here."

Aurea stepped inside and was happily surprised to see Nan walking to her.

"What are you doing here?"

"Thomas and Amanda invited me, and I have some time before classes start up again," Nan said. "We wanted to surprise you."

When Aurea woke up in the hospital two days after Jackson attacked her, Nan was by her side. As soon as Aurea was safe, Thomas needed to go back to South Dakota to be with Adam. He didn't want Aurea to wake up alone, so he called the only number she had saved on her cell phone. Nan answered and was on the next flight to Minnesota. She took two weeks of personal time from her position as Director of American Indian Studies at the university in South Dakota and helped nurse Aurea back to health. They spoke on the phone every day since.

Now, here she was in person. Aurea was touched that Thomas and Amanda would do this for her.

"I'm not just here for you, you know," Nan said and turned to Adam. "I have something for you."

She went to her bag and pulled out a small stuffed animal, a white bison. Adam immediately recoiled and reached for his father. Aurea started to ask Nan to put it away; it was a symbol of Adam's terror. Before she could, Nan sat down on the floor, eye level to Adam, and put the stuffed animal in her lap.

"Those bison you saw, I know they were big and scary. When things are big and scary, we sometimes get the wrong idea about them," she said. "The Native Americans know a lot about bison. We have a lot of stories about them. That's because they're important. The bison kept my ancestors alive."

Adam inched closer, drawn by curiosity.

"A bison means abundance and answered prayers, and a white bison, like this one, is a sacred symbol of hope. It means good things are coming." She held out the toy and Adam slowly took it. "You don't need to be afraid of the bison anymore. Respect them, but don't be afraid."

Aurea's eyes watered as she watched Adam look at the animal. She was awed by Nan's thoughtfulness and understanding of Adam's fears. The sound of a sniffle behind her told her she wasn't the only one who was touched. Aurea walked over and embraced Nan as she stood back up.

Adam slept soundly that night. There were no more dreams of the beastly bison.

Plus, he was no longer needed in The Nothing, now that Sarah had a friend.

Acknowledgments

I send sincere appreciation to my "village" that I leaned on during the crafting of this book, which occurred during the most difficult time of my life with the passing of my father. First, to my husband, Rusty, the love of my life, my rock and fortress, who had to listen to endless ramblings about my work and never complained; my children, Jonathon and Aria, my pride and joy, who will always be the greatest things I've ever done or had; my beautiful sister, Dyanna, who never ignored my texts and was always on hand with encouragement; my squad, Lorrie, Susan, Jodie and Jesse, who kept me sane; and to my brothers, Clinton and Steven, who somehow still claim me.

A note from the author

During the editing and publishing process of Sins of the Father, my own father passed away. It devastated me.

I was always somewhat of a carbon copy of him. When I was about twelve, I even dressed as him for Halloween. He demonstrated a love of reading, though for him it was old Louis L'Amour westerns. He helped me grow my love for writing, and at several points in our writing careers, we even wrote for the same publications. For much of my childhood, he was also a scientist. He taught me how to explore the world we live in and ask questions like "why" and "what if".

I struggled with the question of changing the name of this story. I didn't want it to imply a reflection of my own father, or of the other wonderful fathers of the world. Still, the title fits this story quite well. Plus, the real question remains. Whose sin was it really?

I don't know about life after death. I've searched for answers or proof my entire life, often immersing myself in the themes within this story: religion, metaphysics, and science. I do know about living this life to the fullest. That was something else I learned from my father.

He never got to read this, but he was quite proud of me for writing it. Like all of us, he had his flaws. But his biggest sin was leaving me before I was ready.

I hope you enjoyed reading this story, and perhaps saw hints of the people you love, as well.

Very sincerely,

Sabrina

Sabrina Halvorson is a dark fiction author, radio host, and news reporter. A native of California, she now lives in North Dakota with her husband. Visit her website at SabrinaHalvorson.com.

Made in the USA
Middletown, DE
08 September 2022